Rogue Soldiers

Captain Slade Moran, US Army investigator, is hunting the killer of an officer when he rides into Grey Ridge, having lost the trail of the fugitive. Fresh orders await him at the nearby army post, and he is plunged immediately into big trouble. Seven troopers have recently deserted from the fort – an unprecedented number, and none of them have been caught. Also a young officer has been court-martialled for stealing and drummed out of the army.

After examining the two cases, Moran is up against unscrupulous men, vicious killers and a rogue officer. He'll have to lay his life on the line before he can restore justice.

Rogue Soldiers

Corba Sunman

A Black Horse Western

ROBERT HALE · LONDON

ISBN 978-0-7198-0666-7

Robert Hale Limited
Clerkenwell House
Clerkenwell Green
London EC1R 0HT

www.halebooks.com

Typeset by
Derek Doyle & Associates, Shaw Heath
Printed and bound in Great Britain by
CPI Antony Rowe, Chippenham and Eastbourne

ONE

The land was desolate and barren, a rocky wilderness that was largely uninhabited except for rock grubbers looking for silver or gold – usually old sourdoughs digging eternally to prise wealth from the impervious rocks of Colorado. Captain Slade Moran, riding alone, felt that he was the only human in the whole wide world, and the silence pressing in around him, apart from the noises of travel made by his black horse, drove him to the lowest degree of solitude. As a top operator for the military Special Investigation Department of the Division of Missouri, he was at present engaged on a hunt for Joseph Almeyer, a cavalry sergeant of twenty years' service, who, before deserting his post at Fort Logan, south-west Colorado, had shot and killed his immediate superior Lieutenant Goss. Patrols had searched for the killer but had failed to apprehend him, so Moran had been detailed to the chore of locating him.

Moran was tall and powerful, standing three inches over six feet, with a lean, well-muscled body. He was ruggedly handsome: blue eyes far-seeing, hair almost white, and had a manner that was remote, hard and wary. To men at large his appearance was forbidding; his face and bearing proclaiming to all and sundry that he was not a man any stranger should underestimate. His clothes were trail-worn and dusty; a dark blue suit and a yellow neckerchief tied at his throat; his eyes were shaded by the wide brim of a blue cavalry campaign hat. His boots were dusty but well-made and of good quality leather. A cartridge belt, its holster containing a .45 Army Colt, was buckled around his waist, and his long-distance weapon was an army issue six-shot Springfield carbine.

He had picked up Almeyer's trail in the mining town of Lodestone, where the renegade had killed the local town marshal who attempted to arrest him for shooting a miner in a poker game. Moran had arrived in the town only three hours after Almeyer had fled on a fast horse, and, discovering that the physical details of his quarry and the town marshal's killer were similar Moran decided that they were one and the same man and took up the trail leading into the wilderness. Now he was moving slowly through rough country, the few hoof prints here and there in the dust among the rocks being the only link between him and the man he sought.

Almeyer did not seem to be in a hurry, and obviously cared little about the tell-tale tracks he was leaving. Moran continued intently, trailing the killer's horse into the desolate mountains, trying to guess at Almeyer's destination, but there was no apparent design in the fugitive's wandering, no specific direction being followed, and Moran began to think he was failing in his hunt until he heard a mule calling, a harsh, unmusical sound that echoed through the mountain fastness. The black replied before Moran could prevent it, and hoarse reverberations shattered the silence.

Minutes later, Moran emerged from between two massive rocks and saw a mule standing tethered to a rail in front of a hut. To the right a mine entrance gaped blackly in the sunlight, and Moran tensed when he saw the figure of a man sprawled on the ground in the entrance to the mine shaft. He reined in and looked around alertly, his hand on the butt of his pistol. His gaze passed over the dead man, intent only on Almeyer's tracks, and he saw them leading past the hut to where they had halted in front of the mine shaft. His keen gaze picked out the tracks where they had gone on, heading away to the east, and he realized that his quarry had departed.

Only then did Moran dismount and approach the body. The dead man, roughly dressed in dusty working clothes, was lying on his face. A bloodstain between his shoulder blades showed where he had collected a bullet in the back. Moran looked around again. He trailed his reins and moved cautiously, checking tracks, and soon discovered that his quarry had turned from east to south, into an even bleaker region of the desolate mountains.

Satisfied that his quarry had indeed left the scene, Moran returned to the hut. A glance at the sky showed him that night was only a couple of hours away, the knowledge bringing the decision that it was too late to take up the trail again. He decided to make camp, bury the dead miner and get some rest. He was still on one knee beside the corpse, checking through the man's pockets in an attempt to find some identification, when the sound of a boot on hard rock sent him whirling around, reaching for his pistol. He checked the movement when he found himself confronted by a big man dressed as a miner who was holding a shotgun in his gnarled hands. Two other miners were standing in the background.

'Is Hank dead?' the newcomer demanded huskily.

'He's dead,' Moran corroborated.

'And you're robbing his body, huh? Get your hands up, you back-shooting pack rat.'

'Now hold on,' Moran replied. 'I found him like this when I rode in a few minutes ago. I'm Captain Slade Moran, an army investigator, and I'm hunting an army deserter who killed his troop leader in Fort Logan a couple of weeks ago before heading this way. His tracks are there in the dust, and I suspect he killed your friend.'

'Get your hands up,' the miner snarled. 'You ain't getting away with this. We heard the shot that killed Hank and came over, hotfoot. We've had dealings with claim-jumpers before, and you're caught robbing the body.'

'I was searching him for identification before burying him so I could give the details of his death to the local law in Grey Ridge. I plan to stay here tonight and take up the killer's trail at first light.'

The other two miners came forward. One was carrying a rifle and the other had a pistol in his hand. Both were big, powerful men, stamped with the unmistakable ear-marks of those that spent most of their lives toiling among remote rocks in search of an elusive fortune.

'Is Hank dead, Gaffley?' one demanded.

'As a doornail and we've got the bozo who killed him; caught him right in the act of robbing him. Look in the hut for a rope, Turrell, and throw an end over that tall rock.'

'Hold it!' Moran said quickly. 'I can prove who I am. I've got papers stating what my job is. They were signed by General Sherman.'

'We don't want no truck with papers,' said Gaffley. 'None of us can read. We caught you in the act and we're gonna hang you high.'

Moran could clearly see that whatever he said would be of no avail, and he clenched his teeth on a reply as the man called Turrell hurried into the hut. Gaffley did not move. The twin muzzles of his shotgun gaped steadily at Moran's chest. The shotgun was the most feared of all weapons because of its spread of shot. A single bullet from a rifle could easily miss, but a 12-gauge shotgun cartridge widened its killing circle greatly as the range increased – the probability of missing a target was mathematically impossible. The third miner, armed with a Winchester, moved out to the left and covered Moran from another angle.

'I reckon you're a claim-jumper,' Gaffley remarked. 'Shooting's too good for you, so we'll stretch your neck and leave you hanging as a warning to others of your breed.'

'If you hang me you'll be giving the killer a real chance of getting away with the murder,' Moran protested. 'It's only forty miles to Grey Ridge, so take me there and hand me over to the local law. I can prove who I am. It's not much to ask when a man's life is at stake. I reckon I don't have the look of a claim-jumper, and I'm sure you wouldn't want to make a mistake.'

'Claim-jumpers come in all shapes and sizes,' Gaffley retorted, raising his voice and glancing towards the hut as he shouted: 'Hey, Turrell, what in hell are you doing in there? Bring out that rope and let's get this chore done. I'm hankering for my grub. I ain't had a bite since before sunup.'

Moran noted that the twin muzzles of the shotgun moved slightly to the right as Gaffley threw a glance towards the hut, and he took advantage of the miner's momentary loss of concentration. He set his right hand into motion, reached for the butt of his pistol, and produced the weapon in a blur of speed, simultaneously diving low to his left as he cocked the .45. Gaffley caught his sudden movement and tried to recover from his lapse. Moran rolled once and came up into the aim. His gun blasted and the bullet slammed into Gaffley's right shoulder, its impact throwing the miner off aim and putting him into a twisting fall. The shotgun fired and a whirling load of buckshot hammered harmlessly skywards. Gaffley fell to the ground, but Moran was already turning towards the miner with the rifle.

The man was standing frozen in shock, staring at Gaffley, his mouth agape and his rifle forgotten. Moran got up on one knee, covering him.

'Drop the rifle,' Moran snapped, 'and be quick about it.' He waited until the miner had complied before glancing towards the shack. Turrell was emerging, carrying a coiled rope, and he, too, was badly shocked. He had put his pistol in his belt; he had no thought of resisting as Moran took over.

Moran picked up the discarded shotgun and motioned

10

for the miner who had held the rifle to step clear of the weapon. Turrell obeyed quickly when he was told to disarm himself. He dropped the rope, tweaked his pistol out of his waistband and dropped in on the ground.

'Let's get one thing straight,' Moran said. 'I didn't shoot Hank. The killer I'm hunting did. So you two better take care of Gaffley and then haul him out of here. I'm camping here for the night, and when I'm gone in the morning you can come back and bury Hank. OK?'

'Anything you say, Captain,' said Turrell. 'You don't have to worry about me and Ed. Gaffley's the prickly one. He must eat poison mushrooms, the way he gets his back up. He should have listened to you when you told him who you are.'

'Just get him out of here,' Moran said harshly.

He watched Gaffley get some rough medical treatment, and then the two miners hauled the semi-conscious man to his feet and started back into the rocks. Moran followed them for some distance – they were unaware of his presence – until he was certain they were heading back from whence they came. Then he returned to Hank's mine and prepared to camp for the night. He took care of his horse, knee-hobbling the animal, and then carried his saddlebags into a cluster of rocks behind the hut. He took his horse several yards into the rocks and left it in cover.

After cooking a meal he unrolled his blankets and stretched out behind the hut, his pistol close to his right hand. The sun went down as he closed his eyes and as the surrounding shadows deepened he drifted into sleep. When he awoke, the sun was just clearing the mountains to the east, and he arose to begin a new day that promised nothing different from any of the preceding ones.

He saw nothing of the miners who had shown up the day before, and so he picked up Almeyer's tracks and headed out. He guessed he was about forty miles from the town of Grey Ridge, and although Almeyer's tracks headed in that direction, Moran did not think the fugitive would ride there because ten miles to the east of the mining town lay Fort Grant, and no deserter in his right mind would show himself in a community which soldiers frequented.

Moran took all the precautions he could, for if Almeyer sensed he was being followed he would hunker down behind a rock and shoot from cover. The day passed. Moran made a lonely camp as the sun set, and was up and ready to continue at sunup. Almeyer's tracks continued in the general direction of Grey Ridge, which surprised Moran, but they suddenly disappeared when Moran estimated that he was within ten miles of the mining town.

He checked the rough ground incessantly, riding in circles in the hope of picking up Almeyer's tracks. He found nothing. The killer had taken advantage of a wide stretch of solid rock to ensure that he could not be followed to his destination, and had been careful not to ride through any patches of dust. Moran finally admitted defeat and sat his mount while considering his next move. He decided to ride into Grey Ridge.

The mining town was just a straggling collection of huts and tents around a core of wooden business buildings. There was a one-storey hotel, a saloon, a general store, a bank and a law office. The livery barn was located on the outskirts of the community, which consisted of some three hundred people; mostly miners who were employed by the largest mine in the area. Moran had been through this area before, and looked around from the grey ridge, which gave the little town its name. He noted the addition of several larger houses along the so-called main street, which was practically deserted in the late afternoon, but nothing much had changed the way of life in the town.

With his mind still on Almeyer, Moran rode down to the livery barn and dismounted. An old man was busy carrying buckets of water from a nearby well to fill a drinking trough just outside the front door of the barn. Hearing Moran's approach he paused, straightened, and pressed both gnarled hands to his aching back as Moran reached him.

'Howdy, stranger,' he greeted. 'I'm Walt Hannon, the owner of this here horse emporium. Ridden far?'

'A long, long way,' Moran replied. 'I'm Slade Moran, and I'm looking for a man who might have ridden in some hours ago.' He gave a description of Almeyer. 'Have you seen anyone like him?'

'I ain't seen a stranger in several days.' Hannon shook his head. 'What's your feller done? Is he wanted by the law?' He paused, and then asked: 'Are you a lawman? You sure ain't a miner, by the look of you. You've been a military man in your time, huh?'

'I was in uniform a long time ago,' Moran admitted.

'Cavalry, I'll bet.' Hannon grinned. 'There ain't no mistaking a man who's been in the army. I was in the ranks myself, but that was a real long time ago. 'You got all the earmarks of an officer – captain, I'd guess. Toughest rank in the army, I'd say. A man makes captain he's made something he

13

can be proud of. Captains are the backbone of the army. Say, why don't you mosey along to the law office and have a word with Sheriff Appleby? He might know something about your man. Just because I ain't seen him don't mean to say he ain't around, huh?'

'Thanks, I'll do that.' Moran nodded. 'Take care of my horse and gear, will you?' He produced a silver dollar and dropped it into Hannon's ready palm. 'I'll be around for several days, I guess.'

Moran took his Springfield carbine and saddle-bags from the black and left Hannon holding the reins of the horse as he set off along the street. He looked around intently in the forlorn hope of spotting his quarry, but there was no sign of Almeyer. He stopped off at the hotel and rented a room for the night, intending to head for Fort Grant next morning. He left his gear in the room, locked the door on leaving and continued to the law office.

A big, powerful man was seated at the desk in the office; a sheriff's star was pinned to his shirt front. He was in his middle forties, but had the look about him of being a formidable upholder of the law. His long face was hard, like old leather, his eyes an icy blue, his hair short and iron grey. He looked up from a newspaper, gazed at Moran for some moments and then got to his feet.

'Howdy,' he greeted. 'I'm Sheriff Pete Appleby. Can I help you, mister?'

'Captain Slade Moran, Sheriff, a military investigator. I'm hunting an army deserter, name of Almeyer, who murdered a lieutenant at Fort Logan a couple of weeks back. I tracked him through Lodestone, and found a murdered miner about forty miles north of here, so it looks like he's killed again. He was heading in this direction when I lost his trail about ten miles out. I came on here, this being the nearest community, hoping to drop on to him.'

'Almeyer, you say? What does he look like?'

'Not tall; about five-eight, I reckon. He's dark-haired; was a sergeant. Been in the army about twenty years so he knows how many beans make five. Murdered his troop commander and deserted, for no apparent reason. He was previously of good conduct – clean, sober and honest, as they say in the army.'

'It could be a case of frontier fever,' Appleby mused. 'It doesn't only happen to soldiers – sometimes a miner goes berserk for no good reason and kills one of his friends, no less. And it's no use trying to arrest them. They always go down fighting.'

'I wouldn't know about that.' Moran frowned. 'I'll take Almeyer any way I can – dead or alive.'

'You said you think he killed a miner about forty miles north of here. There are more than a score of rock grubbers out that way. Have you got a name for the dead man?'

'Three other miners showed up while I was checking out the scene. One was called Gaffley, and he named another as Turrell. Gaffley called the dead man Hank.'

'I know those men.' Appleby nodded. 'I'll take a ride out there if they don't show up to report what happened.'

'Then you'd better know what happened.' Moran recounted the incident in which he shot Gaffley.

Appleby listened in silence, and then said: 'I guess I better check your credentials, Captain, just for the record.'

'Sure.' Moran produced his papers.

Appleby looked at them then handed them back, nodding. 'They look OK to me, Captain. Are you heading to the fort to check on their deserters?'

'I've heard nothing about local deserters. Cavalry units usually take care of their own absentees. You might be surprised if you knew the number of soldiers who desert.'

'I've been told about the troopers around here. Colonel Rivington was in only last week, telling me there's been a spate of deserters. Patrols have gone out, but none of the fugitives have been found.'

'They usually get away with it if they can put distance between themselves and the fort before they're missed,' Moran mused. 'Has crime increased around here since those men went missing?'

'I've got enough trouble on my hands to keep me and a couple of deputies busy.' Appleby shook his head. 'With all the silver that's being dug up around here, there's got to be badmen trying to steal it. But I reckon they would be ordinary thieves – nothing to do with the army.'

'I'll be riding out to the fort as soon as I can get around to it. Could be new orders waiting there for me.' Moran turned to the door. 'I'll be in town for a couple of days on the off-chance that Almeyer might ride in. I'd like to wipe the slate clean where he's concerned.'

'I'll keep an eye skinned for him,' Appleby promised, 'and my deputies will check around. It's got to be a habit with us, keeping one eye skinned for deserters, but we don't seem to have had much luck dropping on to any. If they are hanging around – which ain't a good idea for them – then they're taking pains to keep out of sight.'

'I'll stay in touch,' Moran said.

He left the office and walked back to the hotel. His stomach was reminding him it was time for a meal, and he entered the dining room. He ordered a steak with all the trimmings, did full justice to it when it arrived and finished off with apple pie. He sat for some minutes afterwards, his thoughts roving over the incidents of the past two weeks.

Before he was assigned to this particular case he had been down along the Mexican border in Texas, hunting three soldiers who had stolen arms and supplies to sell to Mexican bandits across the Rio Grande, and before that he had operated here in Colorado, searching for a missing army paymaster and his escort of six soldiers. Both cases had been brought to a successful conclusion, and now he had to contend with a deserter who was also a cold-blooded killer.

He cut short his musing and left the hotel to find the sun had set and shadows were filling the street. He needed to check for signs of Almeyer, and he stood for a moment in an alley mouth, looking around to pinpoint the more obvious places a man arriving in town would naturally frequent. He heard the sound of a piano being hammered in a nearby saloon and saw its batwings swinging as townsmen entered for an evening's entertainment. It looked a likely place in which to continue his hunt for the fugitive, and he checked his pistol as he strode along the sidewalk.

He peered in over the batwings and counted over twenty men already in the saloon, although the evening had barely begun. Most of those present seemed to be miners – they were of that type – but he saw several men dressed in range clothes, and wondered what they were doing in town on a weekday evening, until he recalled that this was Saturday night. There were also three soldiers in uniform, in from Fort Grant, standing in a group along the bar, talking intently and ignoring everyone around them.

A couple of poker games were in progress at two of the small tables filling the space in front of the long bar where two bartenders were already busy. A third man stood behind the bar, dressed in a brown suit and wearing a cravat at his throat, adorned with a diamond stickpin that glinted and glittered in the strong lamplight.

Moran let his gaze swing around the saloon, looking for familiar faces, and when he saw a man at one of the tables, wholly intent upon his cards, he felt a slight quickening of his pulse as the man's face touched a chord in his mind and triggered a flutter in his memory. He knew the face, noted a scar on it that ran from the right corner of the mouth towards the right ear. He remained at the batwings while he searched his mind for more information, but nothing turned up, although the scar should have jolted his memory, and he remained studying the man, wondering why he seemed so familiar. He was never wrong about faces. He entered the saloon to cross to the bar.

He watched the man in question, although he did not make it obvious, and saw the man's gaze lift to take in his presence. The man did a double-take, and his expression changed momentarily, until he brought himself under control. Moran paused at the bar, still watching intently, and saw the man lean towards one of his companions and speak in an undertone. The second man glanced quickly at Moran, and then threw down his cards and got up to move to the bar, at the same time signalling to another man nearby to join him.

Moran felt his interest quicken, aware that he had been recognized, but as what; an army investigator or merely as an army man? The man who had moved to the bar was joined by the third man, and, after an intense conversation, the third man strode past Moran and left the saloon. Moran felt the prickling of a sixth sense and prepared for action – all the signs were that he had walked into a situation that could explode into shooting.

TWO

Moran bought a beer and drank it slowly, watching his surroundings with keen interest. The man who had left the card table to stand at the bar was watching his movements closely, but was not clever enough to conceal the fact. After serving him, Moran saw the bartender pick up a tray, load it with a bottle of whiskey and three glasses and cross to the table where the man with the scar was seated. The bartender was questioned and glanced several times in Moran's direction while answering. Moran continued to watch. When the bartender returned he spoke again to the man who had been at the table, and, moments later, that man came along the bar and paused casually at Moran's side.

The newcomer was a complete stranger to Moran – tall, raw-boned, with a thin face, and a pointed chin. His eyes were dark and shifty, his manner showing tension. But he smiled when he met Moran's level gaze, and then leaned both arms on the bar. He was wearing a cartridge belt and pistol, but made a big show of keeping both hands well clear of his waist.

'Something I can do for you, mister?' Moran demanded.

'I'm Jake Toft, and I've got a feeling I've met you before but I can't recall where. Do you know me?'

'I don't reckon so.' Moran grimaced. 'I never forget a face. You're a stranger.'

'You've got the look of a soldier about you,' Toft continued.

'I did a stint, and I could say the same about you. I reckon half the men here were in the army at some time or other.'

'Were you in the cavalry?'

'I prefer to forget about my military service,' Moran straightened and finished his beer.

'Let me buy you another.' Toft signalled to the barman.

'No thanks. I only drink when I'm real thirsty.'

'I didn't get your name.'

'I didn't give it,' Moran smiled. 'It's been a long day, and I'm for turning in.' He left the bar, walked to the batwings and found Toft accompanying him.

'I'm leaving, too,' Toft said, interpreting Moran's glance. 'I work in the office at Doyle's silver mine, and I have to go on duty.'

Moran stepped aside when they reached the batwings; Toft smiled and pushed through them to lead the way on to the boardwalk. Moran joined him, but stepped aside from the doorway and moved into the shadows.

'I don't blame you for being careful,' Toft observed. 'This is a tough town, and anything could happen. You got in today, I guess, huh?'

'Yeah, I rode in from Lodestone.'

'That's another tough community,' Toft laughed. 'See you around, mister.'

Moran watched Toft stride off along the sidewalk and then eased his way through the shadows to the alley beside the saloon. He stood motionless until his eyes became accustomed to the gloom before moving along the alley to a side window, which gave him a view of the interior of the building. He saw the scar-faced man sitting at the table, which was to his immediate left, and studied the man's features again, trying to stir his memory, but his mind remained irritatingly blank.

Minutes passed and Moran remained in position. He tensed when Jake Toft entered the saloon by a back door, and his gaze became even more intent. Toft went to the table and dropped into the seat that he had vacated minutes before. Moran wondered at Toft's behaviour. He had allegedly departed to go to work at the local mine, but here he was reporting back to the scar-faced man. That fact told Moran a great deal, and he settled himself down to await developments. Something was going on and he wanted to learn more about it. He mentally prepared himself for a long wait.

But Toft did not remain long at the table. The scar-faced man listened to his report, and then spoke at some length. Toft listened intently, and when the conversation ended, arose to leave the saloon. Moran left the alley with the intention of following Toft. The man headed along the street at a fast pace, and Moran tailed him to a shack on the outskirts of the town, which was set in a huddle of similar buildings. Lamps were shining in some of the shacks, and there was enough light to enable Moran to stay on his tail.

Toft knocked at a door and was admitted into the ramshackle building. Moran edged in close and risked a look through the undraped window beside the door. He saw Toft, talking with the man he had sent out of the saloon earlier along with two other men. All were dressed as miners – denim pants and short jackets. Toft did all the talking; the others listened intently without interrupting. Moran could hear the buzz of Toft's voice but not what was being said. When Toft left moments later, Moran stepped back around the front corner of the shack and remained motionless in the shadows. Toft headed back along the street and Moran followed him.

When Toft entered the hotel, Moran remained outside and peered through a window. Toft went to the desk and spoke to the receptionist, who shook his head emphatically until Toft produced a wad of paper money and peeled off several notes, which he tossed on the desk. The receptionist snatched them up and placed the hotel register on the counter. Toft opened it, scanned the entries and then turned away. Moran remained in the shadows, and followed Toft again when he emerged from the hotel. He was not surprised when Toft returned to the saloon.

Moran went back to the window in the alley and peered through it to see Toft reporting to the scar-faced man at the small table. When Toft sat down and resumed playing poker, Moran eased away and turned to leave. He had seen enough for one night. But as he stepped out of the alley a man appeared on his left, almost collided with him, and snarled:

'Look where you're going!'

Before Moran could answer, a second man loomed up on his right, and the muzzle of a pistol was thrust against his right side.

'Don't give us any trouble,' said the man with the gun. 'Go back into the alley and we'll enter the saloon by the back door.'

Moran felt his pistol being jerked from its holster and raised his hands to indicate that he would not resist. As he turned and re-entered the alley, a gun was pressed against his spine. He walked through the shadows to the back lots. Both men accompanied him, and one grasped his right arm as they continued. They turned the rear corner of the saloon. Moran saw a man standing in the open back doorway of the building, illuminated by a shaft of lamp-light coming from inside. Moran recognized him by the scar on his face.

'Did anyone see you grab him?' demanded the man with the scar.

'No, Nick. He was watching you through the side window.'

'Bring him in, and don't take any chances. He's got the look of a soldier about him, and he could be from the army, on the lookout for deserters.'

Moran was thrust through the doorway and taken to a flight of stairs, which they ascended. He was led into an upper room furnished as an office. Toft stood there, waiting. He gazed stolidly at Moran without speaking. Moran looked around. There was a large safe in a corner of the room, its door open, and Moran noted that it was stuffed almost to overflowing with stacks of paper money and linen bags bulging with coins. In another corner was a couch, and a desk was situated in front of a window over-looking the back lots, its surface strewn with papers and ledgers. A door in another corner stood ajar, and Moran could see that it was a large store cupboard.

'Hogtie him, Toft,' Nick ordered. Moran was tied hand and foot and thrust on to the couch. 'So talk to me,' Nick continued, glaring at Moran. 'I know your face although I can't place it at the moment, but I reckon you know me from somewhere, so spill it quick and save yourself some real bad trouble.'

'I don't know you,' Moran said quietly. 'I've never seen you before. You must have me mixed up with someone else.'

'Where are you from?'

'Colorado Springs. Our head office is there. I'm a trav-eller for a company that sells everything for mining concerns, from picks and shovels to stamp mills. I'm in this area to see the boss man at Doyle's Mining Enterprises.'

'What's the name of your company?' Toft asked. 'We deal with a number of suppliers, and some of them are located in Colorado Springs.'

'I've worked for Lawlor and Impleman for fifteen years,' Moran explained. 'I was last in this area about eight years ago.'

'We deal with that company.' Toft glanced at Nick, 'We had a letter a couple of weeks ago stating that one of their representatives would be dropping by shortly.'

'So you're on the level, huh?' Nick demanded. The scar on his face looked livid in the lamplight. 'And maybe you are, but I sure as hell have bad feelings about you, mister.

What's your name?'

'Slade Moran. If you have any doubts about me you can always contact head office and check me out. So who are you? I like to know who I'm dealing with.'

'I'm Nick Lannick, and although Pat Donovan owns this place I'm the top man around here. I'll be contacting your head office, Moran, you can bet, and asking for a run-down on you.'

'Are you gonna turn him loose?' Toft seemed disappointed.

'Do you reckon he should disappear without trace?' Lannick demanded, and grimaced when Toft nodded emphatically. 'Then some other guy will arrive, and we'll have to start all over again, but the next time it might not turn out right.' Lannick shook his head. 'Before we turn him loose he'll have to answer a few more questions. I know I've seen him someplace, and I wanta know where before I'm satisfied about him.

'So tell me some more about yourself, Moran. I know I haven't set eyes on you in the last five years, so talk about your doings before then.'

'I was working out of our Chicago office about that time,' Moran said. 'I came back this way only a couple of months ago – promoted to an area manager – and I thought I'd look up some of my old haunts. Like I said, I was last around here about eight years ago.'

'Mike Doyle was in the big seat in the company around that time,' Toft said. 'Did you ever meet him?'

Moran shook his head. 'I don't remember ever seeing Mr Doyle. As I recall, it was Joe Catlin handling the supplies in those days.'

'Yeah, that's right, so he did,' Toft agreed, and his expression changed, as if he began to believe Moran.

'OK, I'm prepared to admit we might have made a mistake about you, Moran,' Lannick said. 'But if I turn you loose now you'd better not run to the sheriff with any complaints about us. Appleby wouldn't do anything anyway, and you'd only bring us back on your neck. Do you understand?'

Moran nodded. 'Sure. There's no harm done. Just untie me, give me my gun, and I'll go on my way as if nothing happened.'

Lannick hesitated for some moments, his expression still showing doubt, but he finally nodded and motioned to Toft.

'Turn him loose and get him out of here,' he said grudgingly. 'You'd better get your business around here done quick as you can and then haul your freight, Moran. I got a nasty feeling about you, and I don't like it.'

Moran did not reply. He remained impassive while Toft untied him, and took his gun when it was handed to him.

'Come and have a drink,' Toft said. 'I'm the man at Doyle's you'll have to deal with if you're selling mine machinery, and a chat now just might save both of us some time later.'

Moran followed Toft out of the office and down to the ground floor, where they passed through an inner doorway into the saloon and bellied up to the bar. Toft bought two whiskies. His manner changed considerably when he talked about the mining industry. Moran answered Toft's questions easily, for he had been well versed in the business before it became a part of his cover

27

story. His immediate superior, Colonel Wakefield, was a brother-in-law to William Lawlor of Lawlor and Impleman, and had arranged Moran's credentials with the company so that any query regarding his identity would be answered correctly.

'So where did you know Lannick before?' Toft asked presently.

Moran shook his head. He was not prepared to admit that Lannick seemed familiar to him. 'I don't know him and that's the truth,' he replied. 'He's a complete stranger to me.'

'He thinks he knows you from somewhere, and you better start hoping there's nothing in your past to tie you in with him.'

'He's pretty damn touchy,' Moran observed. 'How did he get that scar?'

'He doesn't talk about it, and no one asks.'

'He doesn't own this place, huh?'

'No. He runs it for Donovan. That's Donovan along the bar, watching what's going on. A real dandy-Jim, ain't he?'

Moran studied the smartly dressed man at the far end of the bar and nodded. He needed to ask more questions about Lannick, but did not want to show too much interest. He finished his drink and turned to leave, but paused when he found the two men who had taken him out of the alley and up to the office standing close behind him. One of them was holding a two-shot derringer half concealed in his hand. Moran glanced at Toft and saw he was grinning.

'You thought you'd got away with it, huh?' Toft demanded, and now his eyes were unfriendly again, his manner hostile. 'If you've got any sense you'll go with us without trouble, else there'll be a shooting right here in the saloon, and we don't want to scare the customers away, huh? Just walk out of here with us and we'll go somewhere quieter where we can get down to business.'

Moran eased his right hand towards the butt of his holstered gun. Toft laughed.

'Don't bother with that,' he said. 'It was unloaded in the office. Lannick doesn't miss a trick. Now what's it to be? It's your call.'

'OK,' Moran said without hesitation. 'It looks like I don't have a choice. What's Lannick afraid of if he thinks I'm from his past?'

'He's afraid of nothing – just careful,' Toft grinned.

'Where are you taking me?'

'You'll find out soon enough. Just follow Dawber. He'll lead the way, and we'll follow you.'

Dawber, a big man with wide shoulders and a knowing grin on his rough face, turned and walked to the batwings. Moran followed him, and Toft and Smith, holding the derringer, moved in behind. When they left the saloon Dawber turned to the right. Moran was ready to fight, but he needed to find out what was going on, and decided to play along for a little longer. He had no idea what was in Toft's mind, but he expected the end to be the same whatever occurred. They were intent on disposing of him.

'Have you got a horse in the livery barn?' Toft demanded.

'Sure. Are you taking me out of town?'

'Wait and see,' Toft replied.

They reached the stable and Moran saddled his horse.

Dawber covered him with a pistol while Toft and Smith saddled their own mounts. Then they waited for Dawber to do likewise. Moran did not like the idea of being taken out of town, and tensed himself for action. Toft was standing very close, covering him with his .45. Smith was watching Dawber throwing his saddle on a horse. Moran knew he would not get a more opportune moment to resist, and clenched his left hand into a fist. He slammed his knuckles against Toft's chin, grasped the man as he staggered, and snatched at Toft's pistol.

Toft uttered a cry of pain but reacted quickly, pulling his right hand away from Moran and then trying to cover him with the pistol. Moran tightened his grip on Toft and pulled the man around to shield him from Smith, who slapped his holster in a fast draw. Moran twisted the gun out of Toft's hand and thrust him into Smith, at the same time cocking Toft's gun. Smith's gun exploded with a crash. Toft pitched forward on to Smith and they both fell to the ground. Moran stepped away into the shadows, swinging the gun to cover Dawber.

The big man was in the act of tightening the girth on his horse, but straightened quickly and reached for his holstered gun. The echoes of the shot were hammering around inside the barn and gunsmoke was thick in Moran's nostrils.

'Get your hands up, Dawber,' Moran yelled.

Dawber paused, screwing up his eyes to pierce the shadows. He continued to draw his gun. Smith disentangled himself from Toft and sprang up in the instant that Dawber fired at Moran, and the bullet smacked into his chest. Moran took another step to his left as Smith fell again, and, when he saw Dawber swinging his gun to fire once more, he shot Dawber in the right shoulder. Dawber let go of his gun and fell forward on to his face.

Moran exhaled deeply to rid his lungs of cloying gunsmoke. The dim lamplight inside the stable did little more than lighten the gloom but he could see well enough for what he had to do. He went forward, bent over Smith and found him dead. Toft had been hit in the chest by Smith's bullet, but he was still alive but bleeding badly. Moran kicked Smith's gun away and went to Dawber, who was lying on his face. The big man was breathing laboriously. Blood dribbled from the bullet hole in his right shoulder.

Moran heard the sound of approaching voices out front. He put his horse back in a stall and hurried to the rear door of the stable, eased outside into the darkness and flattened himself against the wall beside the door. He peered back into the barn. Two men came running in through the big front door. A law star was glinting on the chest of one of them, and Moran recognized Sheriff Appleby. Moran faded away into the night and went briskly along the back lots towards the rear of the saloon.

Moran's ears were still buzzing from the shooting when he halted against the rear wall of the saloon close to the back door. He slid Toft's pistol into his waistband and drew his own gun to check it. Toft had not lied when he said the weapon had been unloaded, and Moran reloaded the empty chambers before returning it to his holster.

He tried the back door of the saloon and found it locked. Lannick was being very careful, he thought, but not careful enough. The man's actions hinted at some kind of crookedness going on around town, and Moran wanted to know if it involved any of the deserters he had heard about. He recalled seeing the safe up in the saloon office, which was over-filled with cash, and he did not think the saloon business could be that profitable, which indicated that another, probably less legal, project was being run on the side.

Moran needed to talk to Lannick in a situation in which the man would be at a disadvantage; a gun stuck in his stomach should remove the starch from his attitude. Moran went into the alley beside the saloon and peered through the side window, looking for Lannick, but he had not returned to his card game. Moran assumed that he was still in his office and knew this was an opportune moment for doing his duty.

Returning to the back lots, Moran found a window some yards beyond the door of the saloon and broke a pane of glass in it with the barrel of his pistol. He waited some minutes, listening intently, and when he decided that the noise of breaking glass had not been heard he reached inside and lifted a catch, which allowed him to open the window. He climbed through the aperture and found himself in a storeroom. Dim light showed him the hazy outline of crates and kegs. He felt his way along the left-hand wall and reached a door, which opened to his touch, giving him access to a short passage. He mounted the stairs leading up to the office, and drew his pistol when he reached the upper storey.

Lamplight showed through a crack at the bottom of the office door. Moran moved in close and put an ear against the door panel, listening carefully. He heard nothing, drew his Colt, and reached out with his left hand. The door opened easily. Moran entered the office and saw Lannick seated at his desk, working on a ledger. Moran closed the door, saw a key in the lock, and turned it. Lannick looked up quickly and his right hand made an instinctive movement towards a drawer in the desk.

'Don't try it,' Moran warned, his gun pointing at Lannick's chest.

Lannick shrugged and sat back in his chair. The scar on his face looked livid and angry in the dim light. His dark eyes glittered. He was tense, like a cougar preparing to attack.

'So Toft couldn't get you out of town, huh?' Lannick demanded. 'Is he dead?'

'He's barely breathing. Smith is dead, and Dawber took a slug in his right shoulder,' Moran said tersely. 'Now perhaps you'll tell me what this is all about. You recognized me earlier and that triggered off this trouble, which means you're afraid of me for some reason. So who are you and why are you worried about your past? What crookedness are you running around here?'

'I don't know what you're talking about,' Lannick said.

'Don't lie.' Moran moved around the desk, jerked open the right-hand drawer and picked up a gun lying inside. 'Tell me what's going on.'

'Are you a lawman?'

'I've got the gun so I'll ask the questions.' Moran pressed the muzzle of his gun briefly against Lannick's forehead before moving away. 'All I want from you are some answers. Why did seeing me trigger you into setting men on me? They were going to take me out of town and kill me, which tells me a great deal, but I want to know what's going on, and you're going to tell me.'

'You're some kind of a lawman.' Lannick nodded slowly. 'Where have you come from? You've only just arrived in town. I keep a close watch on the comings and goings around here. And you've got the look of a lawman about you.'

Moran could tell that he was going to have trouble with Lannick. The man would not break easily, that was certain, and Moran did not know enough about the setup in town to push for answers. He wondered again where he had seen Lannick before but nothing came to mind. He considered his next move, sensing that he should leave and do some more investigating before continuing this line of inquiry. He decided to back off, and was moving towards the door when someone outside the office grasped the handle and attempted to enter.

'Hey, Lannick, why the hell is this door locked?' a harsh voice demanded. 'What's going on? Are you in there? Open the door at once; I wanta talk to you. The sheriff is down in the bar. There's hell to pay. Some of those hard-cases you employ are lying shot in the stable and Appleby wants to see you now.'

'It looks like you've bitten off more than you can chew,' Lannick grinned. 'So what happens now? I've got you between a rock and a hard place, mister.'

Moran did not hesitate. The man outside the door was rattling the handle impatiently. Moran went behind the desk and struck Lannick with the barrel of his pistol. Lannick gasped and collapsed, his forehead striking the top of the desk as he fell forward. Moran looked around. He had to get out. He turned to the window, opened it and peered out into the darkness. A voice shouted from the dense shadows below, and then a gun crashed. Muzzle flame speared through the shadows and a slug struck the wall a couple of inches from Moran's head. He ducked back into cover, wondering what he had walked into, but he was prepared to shoot his way out if he had to. . . .

THREE

Moran moved quickly to the door of the office. The man outside was calling Lannick insistently while hammering on the door with his fist. Moran cocked his gun. He unlocked the office door, jerked it open, and the smartly dressed man he had seen in the bar earlier staggered into the office. Pat Donovan, the saloon owner, pulled up quickly at the sight of Moran's gun. He glanced beyond Moran and saw Lannick lying unconscious at the desk.

'What in hell is going on here?' he demanded. 'Did you do that to Lannick?'

Moran thrust the muzzle of his pistol into Donovan's stomach. 'Keep your mouth shut,' he rapped. 'Have you got a gun on you?'

'It's in a shoulder holster.' Donovan spoke through his teeth, and held his hands away from his body. 'I don't know what's going on, but I don't want any trouble.'

Moran relieved Donovan of his gun. 'Get down on your belly,' he said.

Donovan took one look at Moran's expression and dropped quickly to the floor. Moran moved to the door.

'Stay where you are until I've left,' he rasped, and departed. He went down the stairs two at a time, and as he reached the passage below he saw two men entering through the rear door. The foremost was carrying a gun in a holster slung low on his right hip. He paused at the sight of Moran, and then reached for his weapon. Moran beat him to it and fired, aiming for a shoulder. The strike of his slug spun the man around and he fell against the second man, who was in the doorway. Moran ran forward. The wounded man was sliding to the floor. Moran struck the second man across the left temple with his gun barrel, pushed him aside as he began to fall. He jumped over both men, and ran out through the doorway.

As he moved across the back lots a voice yelled from the window of the saloon office, and then a gun blasted repeatedly hurling a string of shots into the shadows. None of the slugs came anywhere near Moran and he ran off to the right, making for the stable. He needed his horse, for he intended leaving town until the situation settled down. He turned into an alley beside the general store and gained the street. A number of townsmen were moving around, some attracted to the barn by the earlier shooting and others making for the saloon to check on the latest outbreak.

Moran walked to the livery barn. A group of men were standing in front of the big open doorway, and a man wearing a deputy sheriff badge was lounging against a door post, preventing everyone from entering. A short, tubby man past middle age, wearing a brown store suit and carrying a medical bag, emerged from the barn and paused to speak to the deputy, a big and ungainly man, who carried a double-barrelled shotgun with the butt tucked into his right armpit.

'OK, Clancy, I've got all I need,' said the doctor. 'Send some men in to pick up Toft and Dawber. I want them taken to my office. The other one, Smith, is dead as a doornail. You can inform Walton that he can remove the body. Have you any idea where the sheriff went? I need to give him the details.'

'He headed for Donovan's saloon, Doc,' Clancy replied. 'The three men in here were employed by Lannick.'

'OK, I'll find him. Get yourself moving, Clancy. I need to do some more work on Toft and Dawber before I'll be satisfied with them.'

The doctor departed. Moran remained in the background while Clancy supervised the removal of the wounded men, and when they were carried along the street to the doctor's office the watching townsmen followed like a flock of sheep. Moran walked into the stable, collected his horse from a stall and led the animal out to the street. He rode to the hotel, left his horse out front and went to his room to collect his gear. The hotel seemed to be deserted, and Moran left without seeing anyone. He mounted the black and rode out of town, following the shadowed trail, which he knew led to Fort Grant.

The trail was pale in the faint moonlight. The sky seemed over-filled with countless stars, shimmering and scintillating. Moran pushed on, his mind busy on his experiences in the town. He was tempted to get help from Fort Grant and place Grey Ridge under martial law, but that seemed to be too stringent an action for the situation, although he needed to be able to come and go with impunity if he were to do his duty efficiently. He had lost touch with Almeyer, and needed to get back on the killer's trail. . . .

Fort Grant was situated beside the trail where it cut through a high ridge of grey rock that stretched forbiddingly for miles on either hand. An outer wall surrounded the clustered buildings of the fort and the big gateway was surmounted by a blockhouse, which gave a commanding view of the frontal approach. A lantern was suspended from the gate, and a sentry was standing in the doorway of a guardhouse. The sentry called a challenge when Moran reached the gate and Moran replied with his rank and name. The sentry checked his papers and then waved him through, saying, 'You'll need to report to headquarters, sir. Lieutenant Bamford is the duty officer, and he'll be inside. I'll get a runner to show you the way, Captain.'

Moran was escorted across the parade ground and handed over to the sentry standing before the door of the headquarters hut. Yellow lamplight spilled from many of the windows in the squat buildings around the parade ground, creating little pools of radiance in the dense shadows. Moran dismounted and tied his horse to a post in front of the porch.

The sentry opened the door of the hut for him and Moran entered to find a tall young officer seated at a desk. When Moran gave his rank and name, the lieutenant sprang to his feet and saluted. He was dark-haired and handsome; smartly dressed, a new uniform.

'Welcome to Fort Grant, Captain,' he greeted. 'I'm Lieutenant Bamford. We've had a wire from general headquarters informing us that you were in the area and would be likely to visit us. There are a couple of messages waiting for you, and Colonel Rivington is anxious to talk to you. Are you merely passing through?'

'Right now I'm not certain of my future movements,' Moran replied, 'but I haven't been posted here. I'm with the Special Investigation Department.'

Moran noted a slight change of expression on Bamford's face at the mention of his department, and he wondered if Bamford had a guilty conscience. But the young officer quickly recovered himself and continued.

'Colonel Rivington is the commanding officer, sir. He's asked to be notified of your arrival the moment you showed up. Did you come by way of Grey Ridge, Captain?'

'Why do you ask?' Moran countered.

'The town is off limits to all ranks until further notice, sir.'

'So I'm not the only one to find trouble there, huh?' Moran nodded. 'But no one in town knows I'm a soldier. What's going on around here, Lieutenant?'

'There's a certain amount of friction between our men and a faction of the townsmen in Grey Ridge, although no one seems to know who or what started it. Three troopers have been shot and wounded over the past month, hence the off-limits order. Morale is low at the present time. Men have been deserting, and patrols have not caught any of them, which is unusual. I heard you were pursuing a killer, Captain.'

'All the way from Lodestone, but I lost his tracks on the other side of Grey Ridge.'

'So you rode into town, and found trouble?' Bamford prompted.

'That's right.' Moran considered his experiences in town. 'I had to do some shooting myself, but I'll be riding back to Grey Ridge in the near future, hopefully with a patrol, to force a conclusion. Is the town off limits to all ranks, too?'

'Yes, Captain.'

'But I saw three soldiers in the saloon this evening when I was there.'

Again, Bamford's face changed expression. Then he nodded and smiled, obviously relieved. 'Of course, Lieutenant Ryker rode in on duty with a detail. For a moment there I thought we had some more trouble; it's been quite hectic for the last few weeks. A fire was started deliberately here in the fort, and an outlaw gang has been operating in the county. The bank in Grey Ridge was robbed last month, and there have been two murders. We're sending out patrols but they've found no trouble anywhere.'

'And you think I've been sent here to investigate the trouble?' Moran shook his head. 'I'm hunting a sergeant who killed his troop leader and then deserted.'

'There is another matter that has given us a lot of trouble recently, Captain.' Bamford spoke slowly, as if considering whether or not he should broach the subject. 'Lieutenant Cahill was found guilty of embezzlement and cashiered. It was a bad business, especially as Cahill was engaged to marry Laura Rivington, the colonel's daughter. But you can always catch up on local news, sir. You'd better report to the colonel right away. He has been expecting you, and seemed mighty impatient today because you hadn't arrived.'

'OK, take me to him.'

'He'll be in his quarters now. I'll show you the way.'

They left the hut and Lieutenant Bamford led Moran through the shadows to the officers' quarters, a row of huts towards the rear of the fort. Bamford knocked at the door of the largest hut.

'I'll have an orderly take care of your horse, Captain,' Bamford said, 'and your saddle-bags will be taken to a guest room in the officers' quarters.'

The door opened and a short, heavily built man appeared in the doorway, his badges of rank indicating that he was a colonel.

'Colonel Rivington, Captain Moran,' Bamford introduced, saluting his superior before moving away smartly.

'I'm relieved to see you, Captain!' Rivington stuck out his hand and Moran grasped it. 'I've been expecting you. Come on in and we'll talk.'

Moran entered the quarters and Rivington closed the door. The colonel was in his late forties; his face was weathered to the colour of old leather. His hair was short-cropped and iron grey. His eyes were alert, almost too bright, and his expression showed that he was a worried man. He led the way into his living quarters and went over to a drinks cabinet.

'Sit down. Would you like a whiskey?'

'A small one, please, Colonel.' Moran sat down in an easy chair to one side of a fireplace.

Rivington poured two whiskies and brought a glass to Moran before seating himself on the opposite side of the empty grate. Moran glanced around at his surroundings. The quarters were tidy and clean, and showed a woman's hand in the furnishings and flowers in vases on the window sill and a large table.

'I've heard a great deal about you, Moran,' Rivington said, 'and all of it good. Last year you investigated a missing paymaster with good results, and recently you've been after a killer.'

'I lost his tracks about ten miles the other side of Grey Ridge,' Moran replied, 'and I found trouble in town, which caused me to leave in a hurry. I came here for help, Colonel. I need some men to back me when I go back to Grey Ridge. I have a feeling that my man will be in town, and I need to get him before he can clear the area.'

'The town certainly needs cleaning up.' Rivington drank his whiskey, his alert blue eyes watching Moran over the rim of his glass. 'But your hunt for Sergeant Almeyer will have to wait, Captain. I received a wire from head-quarters stating that you are to look into the trouble we're having around here. I had asked for help, and was informed that you were heading in this direction and I could expect you to call in here. Your fresh orders arrived this morning. I have the wire here. We need a man of your abilities. You've been trained to investigate, and there are some points that need expert handling.'

'I'll do what I can, sir,' Moran replied. 'I heard that you've had more than the average in desertions.'

'That's only a part of it.' Rivington leaned forward in his seat. 'Some money went missing from the office safe and guilt pointed to one of my officers – Lieutenant Cahill. He, unfortunately for us, is the nephew of General Cahill, who has taken an interest in the case. A court martial took place here last week and Cahill was found guilty – the evidence was overwhelming. He was cashiered. But I'm not satisfied. The case seemed too cut and dried. Cahill is a likeable young officer, previously clean, sober and honest. He strenuously protested his innocence. I'd like you to go over the evidence that was presented and see what you make of it because I just don't know what to think any more.'

'I'll study the summary of evidence,' Moran said.

'There was a further complication in the case,' Rivington said. 'Cahill was engaged to marry my daughter. He moved to town to continue, as he says, the fight to prove his innocence and now she has left the post to stay in Grey Ridge to be near him.'

'I'll get down to it immediately.' Moran finished his whiskey and rose. 'I'll have something to eat, find a bed and settle down with the summary of evidence.'

Rivington got to his feet. He shouted for his orderly and a soldier appeared.

'Jones, this is Captain Moran; Special Investigation. He'll use the spare quarters while he's here. Show him in, get him a meal and also collect a summary of evidence of the Cahill case from the Troop Office for his perusal. Then find Trooper Perrin and tell him he's been detailed to take care of the captain, starting now.'

'Yes, sir.' Jones looked at Moran and nodded. 'If you'll come with me, Captain, I'll show you to your quarters.'

Moran saluted Rivington.

'I'll see you again in the morning, Captain.' Rivington acknowledged the salute, and seemed greatly relieved as Moran departed. . . .

*

In Grey Ridge, Sheriff Appleby was a worried man. The shooting at the livery barn had shocked him, and as soon as he could he hurried along to the saloon to remonstrate with Lannick. When he had agreed to work with Lannick it was on the understanding that violence would be avoided. But recently, trouble had increased by leaps and bounds, and now this shooting at the stable, leaving one man dead and two badly wounded, shredded the agreement Appleby had made. Combined with the desertions from the fort, this latest shooting went too far for Appleby's comfort. Among other things, he had a reputation to maintain. He strode into the saloon to look for Lannick.

Donovan was entering the bar from a back room, and Appleby crossed to him.

'You'd better go up to the office, Sheriff,' Donovan said before Appleby could speak. 'There's been hell to pay up there.'

Appleby clenched his teeth and waited for more information, but Donovan shrugged and walked behind the bar. Appleby stifled a sigh and went up to the office. He found Lannick sitting at the desk, looking much the worse for wear, his face pale and showing shock. Blood had dribbled down his face from a large bruise on his left temple. A whiskey bottle stood at his elbow, and Lannick was refilling his glass when Appleby entered.

'What happened here?' Appleby demanded.

'You might well ask,' Lannick spoke through clenched teeth. His head hurt like hell and he felt ill.

'I've just come from the stable,' Appleby said. 'Toft has been shot, so has Dawber, and Smith is dead. They're your

45

men – what were they up to? Whatever it was, it looks like they got the dirty end of the stick. So give it to me straight. What were they doing?'

'There was a stranger in here earlier.' Lannick tried to speak out of the right side of his mouth because the left side of his face, from temple to chin, felt as if it didn't belong to him. 'He looked like trouble waiting to happen. When I first saw his face I figured I knew him from somewhere but couldn't place him, and he looked like he recognized me. I tried to find out who he was, friendly like, but he was hell on wheels. He laid into me with his pistol.'

'What did he look like?' Appleby demanded.

Lannick described Moran and the sheriff cursed.

'Say, that's the guy who came into my office soon after he arrived in town. Said his name was Slade Moran, and showed me papers which proved he is a captain in some military investigation department. He's on the trail of a deserter that killed an officer; lost his tracks about ten miles out and came into town in the hope of spotting the killer.'

Lannick sprang to his feet, then groaned and sank back into the chair, holding his head in his hands. 'I knew I'd seen him before. It was in Colorado Springs last year. He'd just busted a gang that killed an army paymaster and stole a payroll. The newspapers made a big thing of it at the time. That's where I saw him. And tonight I thought he was after me!'

'What have you done that would interest him?' Appleby demanded. 'I know you're crooked as a corkscrew, Lannick, but you never say much about yourself. Now you listen here. I came in with you to make some easy money, and I'll keep my end of the bargain, no sweat. But I won't tolerate killing. You said there would be no bloodshed. Now I've got one dead and two wounded men on my hands, and Toft and Dawber will talk plenty when they can sit up again and take notice. Folks will start asking questions, and I don't want them getting any doubts about me.'

'You worry too much,' Lannick growled. 'There'll be no more trouble, I promise you. We'll lie low until Moran departs before we continue. There was no trouble with the bank robbery here in town, huh? Your cut was plenty big, and there'll be a lot more like that in future. Just keep the law off our necks and you've got nothing to worry about. The boys out at the ranch don't cause any trouble, and they don't come around here.'

'That ex-officer, Cahill, is hanging around,' Appleby mused. 'He makes me feel uneasy. They kicked him out of the army for stealing, and he's moping around town saying he's gonna prove his innocence. If he does manage to do that I guess the only one at the fort who'll carry the can is your brother. He's even more crooked than you, despite his airs and graces and his attempts to live up to being an officer and a gentleman.'

'Don't worry about Cahill,' Lannick shrugged. 'I've talked to him. He ain't a threat to us, and I'll get my brother to take care of him if it looks like he could cause trouble.'

'No more bloodshed,' Appleby warned. 'I won't stand for it.'

'You're getting to be like an old woman!' Lannick shook his head, his eyes cold and hard. 'We'll do what we have to, and that's all I've got to say about it. Now, when's Doyle gonna ship his silver to the bank? Have you heard anything yet?'

'Not a word. But I'll get to know about it in good time.' Appleby paused and thought for a moment, going over the pros and cons of his situation and deciding that he did not like any of it. 'I think I'll take my cut of the bank job right now,' he said. 'I'm quitting, Lannick. I don't like the way this business is turning out.'

'You know the rule.' Lannick spoke harshly, and grimaced when pain shot through his left temple. He pressed both hands to his head but the pain did not subside. 'Nobody takes anything until the whole business is done.'

'That might apply to the rest of your gang but not to me.' Appleby glanced at the open safe in the corner. 'You need to get rid of some of that dough to make room for more.'

'What do you figure you got coming?' Lannick asked.

'Two thousand bucks was the deal.'

'OK, take it out of the safe.' Lannick watched Appleby cross to the safe and bend down at the open door. He reached inside his coat, took a derringer .41 pistol from an inside pocket, cocked it, and held it behind his back. When Appleby turned to come back to him, clutching a thick sheaf of folding money, Lannick said: 'How much you got there? It looks a lot more than two thousand bucks.'

'I took three thousand,' Appleby grinned. 'Call the extra thousand a bonus. I've got to smooth over the shooting that took place in the stable, and I reckon you're still getting away with it pretty damn lightly.'

Lannick exhaled sharply. 'I've got something else for you, Sheriff,' he said quietly.

'Oh, and what's that?' Appleby, noticing Lannick's changing expression, quickly transferred the money he was holding to his left hand and reached for the butt of his holstered pistol. Lannick lifted his gun and triggered it once. The bullet smacked into Appleby's chest and bored through his heart. His life and strength swilled out of him like water running out of an overturned barrel. His legs gave way and he went down like a tree falling to a lumber-jack's axe.

FOUR

Lannick sat motionless at his desk, staring at the body of the sheriff while gunsmoke drifted across the office and the thunderous crash of the shot slowly faded. Heavy footsteps sounded on the stairs and then the office door was thrust open and Pat Donovan appeared, breathing heavily. The saloon owner stared down at the body, his face showing increasing horror as he took in the grim scene.

'Jeez! What the hell happened?' Donovan demanded. 'Was it an accident?'

'The hell it was!' Lannick dropped his gun on the desk. 'He got too greedy, and I could see he wasn't satisfied. He was set to bleed me for all he could get.'

'But he was the sheriff, for Chrissakes!' Donovan leaned against a doorpost and pressed a hand to his chest. 'You'll be the death of me before you're through, do you know that? How are you gonna explain this?'

'I ain't. Get back to the saloon and send Buck Coe up here. If anyone asks about the shot then tell them I was cleaning my gun and it went off accidently. Go on, get moving. I want Appleby's body out of here, fast.'

Donovan gazed at Lannick for an interminable moment, then heaved a sigh and departed. His footsteps sounded uncertain on the stairs. Lannick shrugged and poured himself another drink. He sat staring at Appleby's body until the office door was opened once more and a tall, heavily built man appeared.

'Donovan says you wanta see me, boss.' Coe's gaze alighted on the sheriff's body but his face did not change expression. 'What's on your mind?'

'Get rid of Appleby. Dump him out of town someplace.'

'OK. I'll get a couple of the boys to help me.'

'That's right. Get Weston and Leake, and make it quick. And I want the blood mopped up and the floor scrubbed. You got that? I'm going for supper now, and I want the place done over before I get back. When you've dumped the body you can go along to the law office and ask for Appleby. Tell one of the deputies to get him to come on over when he's got a minute.'

'But—' Coe started to speak, frowning as he gazed at the body, and then he broke off and grinned. 'I get it,' he said. 'You don't know what happened to Appleby, right?'

'That's right. Now get on with it.'

Coe nodded and departed quickly. Lannick leaned back in his seat and massaged his left temple with probing fingers, his thoughts dark and dangerous. That military long-nose Appleby had mentioned would pay heavily for pistol-whipping him. . . .

Moran had a meal served in his quarters by the orderly

51

that had been assigned to him, and then settled down with the summary of evidence pertaining to Lieutenant Cahill's court martial. He read it through as if it were a novel to get all the facts in his mind, and then read it a second time, making notes as he did so. On circumstantial evidence it was obvious that Cahill was guilty. He had been the orderly officer on the day in question – carried the keys to the office and the safe – and no one else had keys or access to the office during the night in question.

Lieutenant Ryker had been the chief witness for the prosecution, and his evidence had given a motive for Cahill's crime – gambling debts run up in Donovan's saloon in Grey Ridge. Evidence corroborating the debts had been given by Nick Lannick, manager of the saloon. It was an open and shut case, and Cahill had been found guilty and discharged ignominiously from the service.

There were no grounds for investigating the findings of the military court, but the intervention by General Cahill on behalf of his nephew, the defendant, was the reason why Moran's hunt for the killer, Almeyer, had been put on the back burner. Moran felt that he would be wasting his time, but the sooner he followed procedure the sooner he would be able to return to his own case. He called for the orderly, and Trooper Perrin appeared in the doorway, wiping his mouth on the back of his hand.

'Find Lieutenant Ryker and ask him to come here, Perrin,' Moran said.

'I can't do that, sir,' Perrin responded. 'Lieutenant Ryker is not on the post. He took a detail into town this morning, and won't be back for twenty-four hours.'

'I've just read the summary of evidence of Lieutenant Cahill's court martial,' Moran said. 'It must have been a shock when he was charged with theft. He had a good record.'

'That's what gambling will do to a man; even an officer, sir.'

'You don't hold with gambling, I take it.'

'That's right, sir. I come from a God-fearing family in Ohio, and learned at an early age to avoid the sins of the world. Lieutenant Cahill was a popular officer. He cared about his men, but his failing let us all down. No good ever came of sinning.'

Moran arose, aware that Trooper Perrin was not the man to ask for background information on the case. He left his quarters and went to the company office. Lieutenant Bamford had just returned from inspecting the main gate guard and was drinking a cup of coffee.

'How did you get on with Lieutenant Cahill?' Moran asked. 'I'm wondering what kind of a soldier he was.'

'We were on good terms, Captain. I like him. He was a fine soldier, and treated his men well. I was surprised when he was charged with theft because he had everything going for him. He was engaged to marry Laura Rivington, and if you meet her you will wonder why Cahill went off the rails. It just didn't add up. He had the world by the tail with a downward pull. He was going places. His uncle is a general, and with that kind of influence he could have gone to the very top. But he had that weakness, and it brought him down in the end.'

'He spent a lot of time in town then?' Moran prompted.

'He didn't appear to. But then it wouldn't take very

long to lose a fortune in Donovan's saloon. I've always thought the games in there were rigged. Lannick, the saloon manager, is little better than a low-down crook and employs some very tough, unscrupulous men. That's why the town has been placed off limits. Soldiers off duty like to drink and gamble, but they don't like being fleeced, and that's why trouble started. As soon as they began to protest they were quelled with violence.'

Recalling the reception he had received at the hands of Lannick and his crew, Moran could understand how the situation had developed, and, having met Lannick personally, it was obvious the man was crooked and deadly.

'You need to talk to Cahill's troop sergeant to get a clear picture of what Cahill was like,' Bamford said. 'Shall I send for Sergeant Braddock?'

'He wasn't called to give evidence but I'd like to see him,' Moran replied. He sat down, and Bamford gave him a cup of coffee. He left the office and returned ten minutes later followed by a big, broad-shouldered soldier wearing the stripes of a sergeant.

'Captain Moran, Sergeant Braddock,' Bamford introduced. 'I'll leave you two to talk. I have to make my round now.'

'Sit down, Sergeant.' Moran motioned to a seat and Braddock dropped into it. He regarded Moran with unblinking blue eyes that were filled with query. 'I'm looking into Lieutenant Cahill's court martial, which seems to be a clear-cut case.'

'He was set up, Captain.' Braddock's powerful voice filled the office and trembled with barely suppressed anger. 'That's why it looks open and shut against him. I

54

wanted to speak up for him at the court martial but the prosecution wouldn't let me. He was rail-roaded, without a doubt, and they've got rid of him, which is what they intended from the start.'

'That's a serious accusation.' Moran studied Braddock's face, and could see vibrant emotion in the man.

'It was a serious charge they worked, sir, and they've ruined Lieutenant Cahill's life.'

'Can you put names to whoever set up the charge?'

'One name is all you need, sir: Lieutenant Ryker!' Disgust sounded in Braddock's voice, but although he spoke fearlessly he shifted uneasily in his seat.

'Keep talking,' Moran said.

'Lieutenant Ryker was jealous of Cahill – hated him because he had everything that Ryker lacked. It was evident to those of us who saw them every day.' Braddock paused and gazed into Moran's eyes for a moment, his anger flaring, but he made a visible effort to control it. 'Is this talk man to man, Captain, and off the record? I'll tell you what I've seen although it can't help Lieutenant Cahill now, but I don't want to put myself in trouble.'

'It's off the record. This is an informal chat to give me some background to the case, and what you say here will go no further. All I ask is that you tell the truth.'

'I'll do that with pleasure, sir. Ryker is a snake in the grass. He stood up at the court martial and swore young Cahill's life away. If it had been a hanging offence then the lieutenant would be dead now. Cahill did play poker, but he wasn't a gambler in the true sense of the word, and I don't believe for a minute that he lost the kind of money they talked about.'

'But the saloon manager gave evidence of Cahill losing hundreds.'

'I don't know how Ryker arranged it, but he and Lannick were in cahoots. I've seen Ryker in town many times, and he was always sitting around in the saloon as if he owned the place. I could never understand it, but they were thick as thieves.'

'So how did Cahill and Ryker get along on duty?'

Braddock shook his head. 'On the surface there was nothing bad between them. They had slight differences of opinion, like all officers do, but I saw what was going on. Ryker hated Cahill, and pulled some mean tricks to drop him in it.'

'You said the charge was fixed against Cahill. Have you any idea how it was worked? There was clear evidence that Cahill was on duty and responsible. He had the keys to the safe and the office. If he was set up then whoever did it had to have a duplicate set of the keys.'

'Ryker had the opportunity to copy the keys when he was duty officer, sir, which all officers do in rotation, and that's what I think happened.' Braddock moistened his lips. 'The keys were copied, and on the night in question, when Lieutenant Cahill was otherwise engaged on his duties, Ryker went into the company office and robbed the safe so the blame would fall on Mr Cahill.'

'Proving that would be difficult under the circumstances.' Moran shook his head. 'All Ryker would have to do is deny it.'

'Nothing was mentioned to the court, but if they knew how Ryker felt and acted around Cahill a different picture would have emerged, and there would have been doubt about Cahill's guilt.'

'Have you any evidence to support your suspicions, Braddock?'

'No, Captain, and that's the hell of it.' Braddock shook his head, his anger vibrant.

'I understand Lieutenant Ryker is on duty in Grey Ridge,' Moran mused. 'I'd like to meet him unexpectedly, if possible. I've been given the authority to handle this case as I see fit. Would you be willing to accompany me to town and point out Ryker to me?'

'I'd go through hell and high water to do that, Captain. I'm your man.'

'And could you pick two or three other men who would back me if we found trouble?'

Braddock grinned. 'I have just the men for the job, sir. They've all suffered at the hands of Lannick's hardcases.'

'Impress on them that they will be on duty. Have them at the stable, ready mounted and armed, in fifteen minutes. I'll give the necessary orders to Lieutenant Bamford.'

'Yes, sir, Captain!' Braddock sprang up, moving fast for a big man, and turned to hurry out of the office. He paused when Moran called him.

'My horse is a black, Sergeant. Have him ready saddled when I come for him.'

'Yes, sir!' Braddock saluted, and departed with a broad grin on his heavy face.

Moran sat motionless for some moments, thinking deeply, and then nodded and got to his feet. He paced the office until Lieutenant Bamford returned.

'Did you have any luck with Braddock, Captain?'

Bamford inquired.

'I'm making progress,' Moran replied. 'I'll be riding back to town in a few moments, and I've instructed Sergeant Braddock to get a detail together to accompany me. We'll probably be gone all night. You can accompany me to the stable and record the names of the men who will be going with me.'

'Certainly, sir. But be warned that you could be riding into trouble in Grey Ridge. Uniforms are shot at on sight.'

'I found trouble when I was there earlier,' Moran replied, 'and I assure you that I was not to blame. But this time I'll be ready for anything.'

'I think you should inform the colonel what your intentions are,' Bamford suggested.

'There's no need.' Moran shook his head. 'I act on my own initiative, and I have the authority to avoid the usual channels. Now let us go to the stable.'

Bamford led the way and Moran followed across the parade ground. They entered the stable to find three soldiers with Sergeant Braddock, and Moran, studying the men by the light of a guttering lantern, saw that Braddock had chosen them well. They were big, hard-faced soldiers with the appearance of being able to handle any situation. Lieutenant Bamford muttered under his breath when he saw them, and frowned as he looked at Braddock.

'Where did you get these men from, Sergeant?' Moran demanded. 'I smell guardhouse about them.'

'Only Trooper Lant, Captain. He came out of the guardhouse last week.' Braddock grinned. 'He was jailed for injuring one of Lannick's dealers in the saloon, and he's been praying for a chance to get back there and settle that business. The other two are Cookson and Deacon. They're good men, despite their appearance.'

'We're not going in looking for trouble,' Moran warned. 'This is a properly constituted military detail. If any of you think you can't obey my orders without question then fall out now. I have to tell you that I am Provost Captain Slade Moran of the Special Investigation Department, Army of the Interior, and I am acting under the highest authority.'

The men nodded. Moran glanced at Lieutenant Bamford, who was shaking his head.

'Take their names and put them on a duty list under my command, Lieutenant,' Moran said. 'As from this moment they're on special duty.'

Bamford nodded, but his expression indicated that he thought Moran was making a big mistake. Moran led his horse out of the stable and swung into the saddle. When his detail joined him he rode to his quarters to collect his saddle-bags and rifle, and then set off towards the gate. They left the fort at a trot and rode back along the trail to Grey Ridge.

At that moment, Nick Lannick was sitting in his office with Lieutenant Ryker, who was in uniform. Ryker, tall and slim, was in his middle twenties; good-looking, with a smooth face and intense brown eyes. He was seated on a couch, very much at ease, with a glass of whiskey in his hand. His voice was low when he spoke.

'So you haven't seen Cahill around for a couple of days,' he mused.

'That's right.' Lannick nodded. The fingers of his right

hand were massaging the big bruise of his left temple. 'But that doesn't mean he ain't around. I've got a man watching him most of the time, but he doesn't have any chance of reversing the verdict of his court martial. No one around here knows that you're my half-brother and that we're working together, so forget about Cahill. He's out of the picture now. And I don't believe he had any suspicion that you were on my side. I'll tell you what I think. You framed Cahill because you wanted Laura Rivington, and now Cahill, the poor sap, is wandering around town like a lost soul, pining for his shattered career. And that Rivington gal is sticking by him. She's moved into town to be near him. I think your actions have pushed them closer together.'

'He won't be around much longer,' observed Ryker, his expression hardening. 'I'm in town on duty with a detail, and Cahill will be dead before sunup.'

'You're going to kill him?' Lannick leaned forward in his seat and placed his elbows on the desk. 'I think that's too soon after his court martial. I've got a big job coming up any time now – the biggest yet – and I don't want any undue activity around town until I've pulled it off. Leave your personal differences until after my job. Then you can kill who you please.'

'You certainly don't take your own advice, do you?' Ryker growled. 'You killed Sheriff Appleby earlier, and that'll raise a stink to high heaven.'

'That was different. Appleby was getting above himself, and it looked like he was gonna start blackmailing me. Anyway, his death will be laid at the door of local soldiers. I've got two men ready to swear they saw a soldier stalking

Appleby. But you could have some trouble coming up.'
Lannick narrated his brush with Slade Moran. 'I didn't
know who he was but he was hell on wheels. He put down
my three men – killed one of them, and then Appleby told
me he was an army captain from the Special Investigation
Department. He disappeared from town and I suspect he's
gone to the fort. Maybe he's been called in to check on
what you've been up to, so you'd better make sure your
tracks are covered. Watch your step, Adam; you could be
up to your neck in trouble right now. Just bear in mind
that I don't want extra trouble at this time, huh?'

'It's OK!' Ryker smiled. 'I've covered myself pretty
good. I'm going back to the fort in the morning, and I'll
soon find out what's going on. You attend to your business
and I'll handle mine, OK?'

'I don't know why you stick with the army.' Lannick
shook his head. 'You'd make a lot more dough coming in
with me.'

'I like the power.' Ryker smiled. 'We work pretty good
the way things are. I'm leaving now to set up Cahill for the
last time. All you've got to do is take care of my alibi.
That's all I ask.'

'Consider it done. You were here in my company all
evening until midnight, and I have several witnesses to
prove it. But be careful. Make a wrong move now and a
whole lot of my business will flop.'

'I'll be back later.' Ryker ignored the advice. He arose,
picked up his hat and left the office to enter the bar. He
paused in the doorway for a moment to look for his detail;
three troopers in uniform. Two were standing at the bar,
drinking, and the third was sitting in a poker game.

Trooper Mason was raising a glass of beer to his mouth when he saw Ryker approaching, and nudged his companion, Snark, hissing a warning out of the side of his mouth.

'Here comes, Ryker.'

'It's about time,' replied Snark. 'Why does he want us hanging around?'

'You know what officers are. And what are you grumbling about? You've got it easy, running around for Ryker. He's a clever man.'

'Too clever.' Snark finished his beer. He was small-boned, muscular and deadly. He had enlisted in the cavalry to escape a murder charge, and was well concealed in the ranks. He carried a hunting knife in a scabbard beneath his shirt, and preferred to use the deadly blade at close quarters instead of the .45 Army Colt he wore in his holster.

'Go and pull Cawston out of that poker game,' Mason continued. He was built like a stone wall, over six feet tall with shoulders that looked three feet wide. He had massive muscles and prodigious strength; he carried a lot of weight and threw it around carelessly. 'Ryker said he wanted to get moving soon as he came down from the office, so jump to it.'

Snark was still grumbling as he crossed to the table where Cawston was seated. He waited until Cawston looked at him and then jerked his head towards the bar. Cawston nodded and threw in his hand. He picked up his ante and stuffed it into a pocket. He was medium-sized, and his good-looking features were marred by a scar which started under his right eye, meandered across the bridge of his prominent nose, and ended above his left eye. They went to the bar.

Ryker stood before Mason. He looked all three over intently, and nodded.

'Time to go,' he said. 'You know what we're gonna do, so let's get to it.'

'Cahill hasn't been around here this evening, sir,' Mason said. 'We've kept an eye open for him.'

'I know where he'll be.' Ryker fought down a pang of jealousy. 'We're gonna have to wait until he leaves Laura Rivington before we can touch him because I don't want that girl to see or hear anything. So button your lip and come on.'

The three troopers followed Ryker out of the saloon and they all walked along the sidewalk to the brightly lit hotel.

Moran halted by the livery barn when he reached the outskirts of Grey Ridge. He dismounted and handed his reins to Braddock.

'Leave the horses in the rear corral,' he instructed, 'and don't off-saddle them. We may need to leave in a hurry. 'I want to talk to Laura Rivington first off, so you'll accompany me, Braddock, and you other three will wait outside the hotel in case I need you. If you see any of Lieutenant Ryker's detail, just don't let them see you.'

Braddock and Lant led the horses away. Cookson and Deacon remained with Moran, and when Braddock reappeared they went forward in a tight group along the street to the hotel. Moran paused at the mouth of the alley at the side the hotel and glanced into its dark anonymity.

'You three can wait in the shadows there, and be ready

for anything,' Moran said. 'Keep out of sight and do not make any noise. The sergeant and I will stick together. He'll be my link with you three. Come on, Braddock.'

Moran led the way into the hotel lobby and as they approached the reception desk, where a short, thin, middle-aged man was seated, Braddock reached out, grasped Moran's arm, and steered him quickly through a doorway on the left, which led into the fairly crowded hotel bar.

'What's the problem, Sergeant?' Moran demanded.

'Lieutenant Ryker is standing at the desk, sir,' Braddock said promptly. 'We would have bumped into him in another moment, and you said you wanted to come on him unexpectedly.'

'Is he in uniform?' Moran demanded.

'Yes, sir, but he's half-concealed by a big potted shrub standing beside the desk.'

Moran eased forward into the doorway and peered around the lobby. He was just in time to see a uniformed officer ascending the stairs at the far end of the lobby.

'It looks like we're just too late to get to Laura Rivington before he does,' Moran observed. 'Stay here, Sergeant, in case any of Ryker's men are hanging around. I'm a stranger here so I can move around freely. I'll see what I can find out about Ryker's business, and I'll come back to you.'

Moran went into the lobby and approached the reception desk. He walked past with the intention of following Ryker, but the man behind the desk called to him.

'Where do you think you're going, mister?' he demanded.

'I'm visiting a friend,' Moran replied, and kept moving.

'Who is your friend?' the man persisted.

'That's none of your business.' Moran's stride did not falter.

'It is my business,' the man said in a louder tone. 'Stop or I'll put a bullet in you.'

Moran glanced over his shoulder and saw a pistol in the man's hand, its muzzle pointing at him. He walked back to the desk with the gun muzzle gaping at him. . . .

FIVE

'We don't permit strangers to wander around this hotel unchecked,' the receptionist said firmly, waggling his gun. 'Check with me first and everyone will be happy. Who is your friend?'

'That is none of your business,' Moran replied. He leaned against the desk and reached out quickly with his left hand, closed his fingers around the barrel of the gun, and wrenched it upwards with a sharp twist that tore it from the man's hand. He tossed it on the floor behind the desk, his narrowed eyes holding the man's intent gaze. 'For your information I am a guest in this hotel. I rented a room when I came into town earlier. Check your register and you'll find the name Slade Moran in room number eleven. Now tell me, does that give me the right to come and go as I wish, or doesn't it?'

The receptionist looked in the register, checked the details, and nodded.

'I am sorry, sir. I was not on duty when you arrived. We have to be careful these days. Please accept my apology. It won't happen again.'

Moran laughed. 'You make damn sure it doesn't,' he said.

'I'm only doing my job, sir.' The man shrugged.

'What's your name? I may want to talk to the manager about you.'

'I'm Charles Regan. I am the manager, sir.'

Moran shook his head and turned away. He ascended the stairs and walked along the corridor to his room. Lieutenant Ryker, standing at a door one along from Moran's room, was knocking on the door. Ryker glanced towards Moran but was fully occupied at the door, and, as Moran unlocked his own door he heard Ryker call out:

'Come on, Laura, I know you're in there. Open the door. I need to talk to you. I know you don't think much of me because of Cahill's court martial, but there was nothing I could do to help him then. Now something has come up that could affect him badly, and I need to talk to him about it – warn him. There are men in town that could give him a load of trouble, and he needs to know about them.'

Moran entered his room and closed the door. He wondered if Laura Rivington was in her room with Cahill. He could hear Ryker's voice getting angrier and angrier as he lost his impatience. Then there was a crash and the sound of splintering wood. Moran opened his door and looked out into the passage. Ryker had smashed his way into the room and was not to be seen. A woman's voice protested loudly inside the room. Moran assumed that it was Laura Rivington, and walked along the passage to peer into the room.

A woman was standing by the foot of the bed. She was

alone apart from Ryker, who was very close to her. Moran saw at a glance that the woman was tall, slender and beautiful, despite the fear expressed on her face. Ryker was talking without pause, trying to talk over her while she protested strongly at his presence.

'Listen to me for a moment,' Ryker shouted. He took hold of her by the upper arms and shook her. She was trying to twist out of his grasp when Moran spoke loudly, and her eyes widened when she saw him.

'What's going on here?' Moran demanded.

Ryker turned instantly, and demanded: 'Are you looking for trouble?'

'I'm not,' Moran assured him, 'but you are certainly inviting it.' He glanced at the woman. 'Is this officer bothering you, Miss?'

'He forced his way in here,' she replied in a trembling tone, 'and I have made it clear that I do not wish to talk to him.'

'You heard the lady,' Moran said to Ryker. 'Just leave, and do try to act like an officer and a gentleman.'

'Go to hell!' Ryker snarled. He came towards the door angrily and raised his hands to push Moran out of the doorway. Moran swayed back from the waist and Ryker's hands missed their target. Moran thrust against Ryker's chest with his stiffened right hand, thrust him sideways, and, when Ryker cursed again and reached for his holstered gun, Moran clenched his left hand and punched him in the stomach. Ryker gasped and dropped to his knees. Moran reached down and took Ryker's pistol from its holster.

'Get up when you are able and move out,' Moran said.

'You can pick up your gun later from the desk in the lobby.'

'Whoever are you, mister,' Ryker gasped, 'you'd better get out of here.'

'I'm not going anywhere. I've come to talk to Miss Rivington and I wish to do it in private. Get up and get lost.'

Ryker struggled to his feet, anger showing in his face, his eyes bright with rage. He pressed both hands to his stomach. Moran sensed that Ryker was considering another attack, but Ryker thought better of it and staggered out of the room. Moran stood in the doorway and watched his departure until he began descending the stairs to the lobby.

'I'm indebted to you,' Laura Rivington said in a low tone. 'But I'm afraid you have made a bad enemy of Lieutenant Ryker.'

'I'm Captain Slade Moran, a special investigator for the army,' he replied. 'I arrived at the fort earlier and found orders waiting that gave me the authority to examine the findings of Lieutenant Cahill's court martial. I've come to talk to you, and I hope you can tell me where I might find Mr Cahill.'

He saw animation flow into her face. Her lips parted and her eyes gleamed. 'I wrote to General Cahill, Richard's uncle; without Richard's knowledge and consent, I might add,' she said. 'Has the General sent you to do something on Richard's behalf?'

'I believe he has had a hand in my change of orders. I've read Lieutenant Cahill's summary of evidence, which is wholly circumstantial, and I have found some flaws in the case. Now I need to talk to Cahill before I approach the prosecution witnesses.'

'You're the answer to my prayers,' Laura said. 'Poor Richard is at his wits' end but he's completely at a loss. He was well and truly set up, and they did not miss a thing.'

'Do you believe he is innocent of the charges brought against him?' Moran asked.

'I certainly do. A grave miscarriage of justice has been perpetrated against him, and one man is responsible for the predicament Richard finds himself in. I do hope you will be able to help him.'

'So where can I find him?' Moran asked.

'I'll take you to him. He no longer stays in the hotel. He was asked to leave, and is lodging in a guest house along the street.'

Moran escorted Laura Rivington down to the lobby. He paused at the reception desk, and saw a shadow flit across the face of Charles Regan, but proceeded merely to report the damage to Laura's room. Regan promised to have it repaired. When Moran placed Ryker's pistol on the desk Regan raised his eyebrows but made no comment.

'The gun will be collected later by Lieutenant Ryker,' Moran said, and continued to the street door with Laura Rivington hurrying at his side.

As they passed the saloon bar Sergeant Braddock emerged from it and followed them closely. Moran acknowledged Braddock's presence with a nod. When he reached the sidewalk, Moran halted abruptly, for Lieutenant Ryker was standing before the door, flanked by three tough-looking troopers. Ryker was poised for trouble and came forward quickly to confront Moran, who noticed that the three soldiers were holding their pistols and looked as if they were prepared to use them. Ryker grinned, his eyes filled with triumph.

'This is as far as you go, mister,' Ryker rapped, spitting out the words as if they were burning his mouth. 'You'll be taught some manners now. Snark, take his gun.'

Sergeant Braddock, half-concealed by Moran, came forward to Moran's left shoulder as one of the troopers moved in on Moran. Ryker gazed at Braddock in astonishment.

'What the hell are you doing in town, Sergeant?' Ryker demanded.

Braddock looked at Moran, who motioned him to remain silent. 'I'll answer your question, Lieutenant,' Moran said quietly. 'Sergeant Braddock is here on special duty under my command; three troopers waiting in that alley mouth form the rest the detail.'

'Under your command?' Ryker demanded.

When Moran gave his particulars, Ryker came to attention and saluted. His face was expressionless.

'I'm Lieutenant Ryker, at your service, Captain,' he rapped.

'You have some explaining to do,' Moran rasped. 'I want to know what you're doing running wild around town in uniform, acting like a drunken trooper and giving a first-class performance of what I assume to be your true nature. You terrorized Miss Rivington in her room – no doubt she will acquaint the colonel with that fact. You attempted to strike me, and, not being content with that, you've waylaid me with three troopers who seem to be prepared to attack me on your orders. Get to it, mister. Tell me what's going on.'

'The town is out of bounds to the military, sir, so we tend to take a strong attitude to all comers. I had no idea you hold a commission, Captain. I assumed you were someone working for the badmen of this town, and I apologize for my attitude.'

'Why were you terrorizing Miss Rivington?' Moran demanded.

'I needed to know the whereabouts of Richard Cahill and Miss Rivington would not tell me.'

'I'm not surprised, Lieutenant. Your behaviour was uncivil and aggressive. I shall be making a report of this incident when I return to the fort. Why are you still in town? Have you accomplished the duty that brought you here?'

'Yes, sir.'

'Then why are you not on your way back to Fort Grant?'

'We were on the point of leaving, sir.'

'I find that hard to believe. But you will leave now, and report to the duty officer at the fort on your arrival. I shall want to know the exact time of your return there. I'll talk to you again in the morning. In the meantime you will confine yourself to the fort until further notice, and hold yourself ready to face me when I return. Now get out of my sight and take your detail with you. Sergeant Braddock, make a note of the names of these men. I'll want to see them later.'

Ryker, pale-faced and stiff-lipped, saluted Moran and turned away, followed by his three troopers. They moved rapidly along the boardwalk in the direction of the livery barn.

'Don't let them catch sight of you, Braddock,' Moran said, 'but I want you to see them out of town. Lieutenant Ryker will face charges if he does not follow my orders.'

'Yes, sir!' Braddock saluted, and permitted a smile to show briefly on his fleshy face. 'Any orders for my detail, Captain?'

'Not at the moment. They will remain in concealment until you collect them.'

Braddock saluted again and departed.

Moran turned to the silent Laura Rivington. 'Shall we continue, Miss Rivington?'

She drew a deep breath before answering, and her voice was shaky when she agreed.

'That seemed a very dangerous moment, Captain Moran. I know Lieutenant Ryker well, and I wouldn't trust him an inch. You must watch him closely after this. He never forgives or forgets. I felt certain he was about to have you beaten by his men, and most probably taken out of town and shot.'

'He'll be watched closely after this,' Moran replied. 'Let's get on and talk with Richard Cahill.'

Sergeant Braddock followed Lieutenant Ryker and his men towards the livery barn, keeping well back in the shadows. He could hear Ryker's voice talking harshly to the troopers, although he could not make out what was being said, and when one of the men turned abruptly and came back along the sidewalk, Braddock had to fade into an alley to avoid a confrontation. The man, Cawston, a hardcase with a record of violence and drunkenness, went past the alley at a fast pace. Braddock slipped out of cover and followed closely, concerned for Moran's safety.

73

Cawston passed the hotel and kept going. Braddock, following, could see Moran and Laura Rivington ahead, walking slowly. When Cawston drew his pistol, Braddock tensed and closed in quickly, pulling his gun from its holster. Cawston levelled his Colt at Moran and Braddock hurled himself forward, striking at Cawston's forearm with the barrel of his pistol. Cawston dropped the gun and whirled around. Braddock slammed his gun barrel against the side Cawston's head and the big trooper bent at the knees and sprawled full length on the boardwalk.

Moran heard the commotion and looked round. He spoke to Laura Rivington and then came back to where Braddock was standing.

'What's going on, Sergeant?' he asked.

Braddock told him, and pointed to Cawston's gun, lying on the sidewalk.

'So that's the way the wind blows,' Moran mused. 'Did you actually hear Ryker give a direct order for an attack to be made on me?'

'No, sir. Although I heard the lieutenant talking, I was too far back to catch what he said. But Cawston wouldn't have come back without a direct order, sir.'

'Get him up and bring him along. We'll check on Ryker later.'

Braddock dragged Cawston to his feet and shook him violently to bring him back to full consciousness. Cawston was big, but Braddock was slightly larger. He pressed the muzzle of his gun against Cawston's spine and urged him to follow Moran, who returned to Laura Rivington. The girl was shocked by what at occurred.

'This is where Richard is staying at present,' Laura said

74

when they reached a house toward the end of the street.

'Please go in and fetch him while I have a few words with Cawston here.'

Laura entered the house and Moran turned to Braddock, who was menacing Cawston with his pistol.

'What's going on, Cawston?' Moran demanded.

'I refuse to answer that question on the grounds that it would incriminate me, sir,' Cawston replied.

Braddock twisted the muzzle of his gun into Cawston's back. 'Answer the question,' he said roughly. 'You're in a load of trouble, Cawston, and there's only one way out for you. Speak up loudly and clearly. The alternative is twenty years in the stockade.'

Cawston did not reply. He stood looking down at the boardwalk, his face shadowed by the darkness. Moran could sense the defiance in the man's attitude.

'Hold him here, Sergeant,' Moran ordered. 'I need to make contact with Richard Cahill now, but I'll cut it short and we'll put Cawston in the town jail until we're ready to return to the fort. Then we'll make sure Ryker and the others have left town.'

'Cawston will be here whenever you want him, sir,' Braddock said easily. 'Get over by that wall, Cawston, drop to your knees and place your hands on your head. If you so much as blink I'll bend my gun barrel over your thick skull.'

Moran entered the house. Laura Rivington was talking to a motherly-looking woman. A tall, broad-shouldered man of around twenty-five who Moran assumed was Richard Cahill was descending a flight of stairs. Laura turned when Cahill called her name, and ran to him as he came off the bottom stair, talking excitedly as he put an arm around her shoulders. She came forward with him, and her voice was melodious when she introduced him to Moran. They shook hands.

'I'm pleased to make your acquaintance, Captain,' Cahill said. 'So you're going to look into my case, I hear. I've learned a lot about Lieutenant Ryker since I've been in town, and none of it is pleasant. He manufactured evidence against me, although I cannot as yet prove that.'

'We'll get together as soon as possible,' Moran replied, and explained his meeting with Ryker. 'Will you hold yourself ready to talk to me when I'm available?'

'With the greatest of pleasure, sir! Is there anything I can do to help you?'

Moran shook his head. 'There's nothing that Sergeant Braddock and I cannot handle,' he said. 'I'll be in touch as soon as I can.'

Moran departed quickly to find Braddock standing motionless in the shadows outside the house with Cawston kneeling passively in front of him.

'On your feet, Cawston,' Moran ordered. 'Head for the law office.'

Cawston arose and walked on along the boardwalk. Braddock remained close to his prisoner, his gun jabbing against the trooper's spine. The law office was a two-storey brick-built building with a large sign outside declaring its presence. Braddock pushed Cawston in through the doorway with Moran following closely.

They entered a large room, which contained a desk, four chairs and two metal filing cabinets. Beyond the desk, against the back wall, was a barred space which served as a cell. A big-built young man was seated behind the desk, a law star glinting on his shirt front. He looked up, gazed at them for a moment and then got to his feet. He was wearing a red check shirt and a leather vest. His feet were encased in high-heeled riding boots. A cartridge belt was buckled around his waist, its holster filled with a long-barrelled Colt, which sat low on his right hip. He was hard-faced, sharp-featured and looked efficient and capable. His blue eyes were bright with alertness.

'Howdy,' he greeted in a hoarse tone. 'I'm Deputy Sheriff Mike Davis.'

Moran introduced himself. 'I spoke with the sheriff when I called earlier,' he added.

'Sure,' Davis nodded. 'Pete told me about you. You're a military policeman, huh?'

'Something of that sort. I have a prisoner I'd like to put in your cells while I attend to other business. Would you hold him for me until I'm ready to return to the fort?'

'Is he drunk?' Davis demanded. 'I'll need a reason for holding him; for the record.'

'Not drunk,' Braddock said. 'He attempted violence against the captain.'

Davis nodded. 'That's as good a charge as any. Lock him in the cage, Sergeant, and I'll keep an eye on him.'

Braddock pushed Cawston inside the cell, closed and locked the door – the key was already in the lock – and handed the key to Davis. Moran thanked Davis again and departed. Braddock followed closely, holstering his pistol. They paused on the sidewalk.

'What now, Captain?' Braddock asked.

'We'll check that Ryker has left town as ordered.'

Moran stood for a moment, looking around into the shadows. Braddock waited respectfully. 'There's some kind of a situation in town,' Moran mused. 'I can almost smell it, although I can't put my finger on it as yet. But it is there, and it intrigues me.'

'Lieutenant Ryker seems to be thick with those men running the saloon,' Braddock said. 'I keep my eyes open when I'm around town, and I see things that most folks miss. Pat Donovan owns the saloon, but he's got a man called Lannick in as a manager, and he has a number of hardcases hanging around like bodyguards. They're the ones who've caused all the trouble for us soldiers.'

'I've met Lannick,' Moran said. 'He set three of his men on me when I arrived. One was killed and the other two were shot. They planned to take me out of town and kill me.'

Braddock whistled through his teeth. 'Is that why Ryker was planning to take care of you just now, Captain?'

'That could be the reason, and if it was then he must be hand in glove with Lannick, and such an association would put a different interpretation on Lannick's evidence given at Lieutenant Cahill's court martial. Let's get down to the stable and check on Ryker.'

They moved, senses alert, through the shadows until they reached the near corner of the stable, where Moran halted.

'Stay here and be ready for anything, Sergeant,' he said. 'I'm going in the back way to look around before showing myself. If Ryker and the others have left then I'll have a better idea of what's happening, but I have a feeling they'll still be around, waiting for Cawston to return. Watch the front door. I'll come out for you if there's no one around. If there is shooting then you'll have to handle it as you think fit.'

'Yes, sir.' Braddock moved into deeper shadow as Moran went along the side of the stable.

Moran slid around the rear corner of the building and eased towards the back door, which stood open, gaping darkly. He pressed against the doorpost while he looked around and listened. He was unable to see anything in the shadows, and heard only the stamp and movement of horses within the building. From his position he could see a lamp hanging over the big open front door, which cast a yellow pool of brilliance across the threshold.

Moran could see nothing suspicious inside the barn but his instincts never played him false, and they were warning him that all was not as it seemed. Ryker had acted strangely, not at all in the way an officer was expected to conduct himself, and the way he had treated Laura Rivington was inexcusable. Moran suspected that Ryker was living under a great deal of tension, and until he knew the reason for the man's actions he was not prepared to give him the benefit of any doubt.

He entered the rear of the barn and stood with his back against a wall, listening intently. One or two of the horses inside seemed restless, and Moran wondered if it was because they could sense men hiding in the shadows. Just then a rider dismounted outside the front door and entered, leading his horse, which he took into a stall nearer the front of the barn. There was a sudden exclamation, and then a man's voice, raised in alarm and anger.

'What in hell are you doing in here in the dark?' the

voice demanded.

Another voice replied in an undertone, which Moran could not properly hear, and then Moran heard a thud and a cry of pain before silence settled once more. Some moments passed and then a voice, which Moran recognized as Ryker's, cut through the tense silence from another position.

'What in hell is going on over there? Who came in with that horse?'

'I don't know, sir. He walked into the stall where I was waiting and I had to hit him.'

'Change your position now and keep quiet. We'll get away as soon as Cawston returns. I'm wondering what the hell is keeping him. I haven't heard any shooting.'

'I'll go check on him if you like, sir.'

'No. Stay quiet and keep your wits about you. I want that long-nosed captain taken care of. There'll be hell to pay if he gets back to the fort and makes a report. We'll take him out of town, kill him, and bury him where he won't be found. Then we can relax.'

Moran dropped a hand to the butt of his gun. So Ryker was prepared to commit murder. He drew his weapon, and the clicks that sounded as he cocked it seemed overly loud in the heavy silence that ensued.

'Ryker,' Moran called. 'This is Captain Moran. I've heard enough to give me a reason to take action against you. Cawston is in jail for trying to shoot me, apparently on your orders. You have the chance to surrender yourself now. You and your men can throw down your guns or resist. I've got the front covered and you can't escape.'

Silence followed Moran's echoing voice and he waited,

crouching, ready for action. Then Ryker's reply came. A gun flashed and hammered and a bullet thudded into the back wall close to Moran's head. An instant later two more guns joined in and began shooting rapidly, filling the barn with the lethal crackle and snarl of flying lead. Gunshots boomed and echoed, reverberating like thunder as a fight swiftly developed.

SIX

The shooting rattled loose boards in the barn. Gunsmoke drifted and slugs thudded into the wall around Moran. He heard bullets smacking near his head but triggered his Colt steadily, his eyes narrowed against flaring light as he fired at opposing gun flashes. He changed position quickly, keeping low, hoping Sergeant Braddock would not rush in and get himself killed. He could hear Ryker shouting orders, but the crashing shots buffeted his voice and bludgeoned the sense of what he was saying.

Moran was not surprised by Ryker's attitude, but could not understand why the three men forming Ryker's detail were prepared to commit murder on their officer's orders. What kind of a situation existed here in Grey Ridge? His thoughts ran unchecked as he traded shots with the three guns shooting at him. There was no sign yet of Sergeant Braddock taking a hand in the incident. Moran moved position and ducked behind a grain bin. He dropped to one knee and paused to reload his smoking pistol.

A lull evolved in the barn and Sergeant Braddock shouted powerfully from the cover of the open front door.

'Captain, where are you? I don't want to shoot at you. Sing out so I can pinpoint you.'

'I'm back here, Braddock,' Moran replied, and fired a shot to one side to mark his position. He ducked as more lead crackled around the bin, then raised up slightly and took quick aim at an answering gun flash. He squeezed his trigger, and thought he heard the tail-end of a yell of pain but could not be sure; his ears were filled with the report of his shot. But he noticed that one of the three guns had dropped out of the fight. At that moment a gun opened fire from the front door of the barn, and he guessed Sergeant Braddock had joined the ruckus.

One of the two guns seemed to be working its way forward to where Moran was waiting, his gun uplifted and ready. He held his fire, content to let Braddock swap lead with the second gun, which was now firing steadily in the sergeant's direction. Moran changed position again, sneaking away to the right to prevent his antagonist from outflanking him. He paused in a corner of the barn and waited patiently, aware that Ryker could not stand and fight because the local law would be arriving soon to check on the disturbance.

The shadows were deceptive with gun flashes flaring and dying, but Moran watched the gun slowly approaching him. He could see no movement beyond the flashing gun muzzle, and avoided looking directly at it to avoid being dazzled. The gun fired again and a bullet smacked into a metal object before screeching away across the barn. Moran triggered two quick shots, and dropped down when an answering shot plucked at the brim of his hat.

It had been close, Moran was aware, and he cuffed

sweat from his brow with his left forearm as he narrowed his eyes in an endeavour to see something of the man behind the gun. Then the thunderous echoes of the shooting abated again, and Moran heard the creak of a door opening and then slamming. He reared up, aware that the sound came from where his adversary was crouching, and it struck him that there was a side door which someone had used to get away from the fight.

Moran sprang up and lunged forward. He caught a glimpse of starlight outside as the side door rebounded slightly under the force with which it had been slammed. He hit the door with his left shoulder and dived low as he passed through the doorway. A gun blasted three shots from close by, the slugs passing closely over him. He hit the ground hard and rolled back against the wall, hearing the click of a gun hammer just ahead as it struck an empty cartridge. He regained his feet and looked around. A figure was running away, illuminated now by faint starlight. Moran halted and threw up his gun, taking quick aim. He fired twice, but his hammer struck an empty chamber after the first shot and he dropped into cover to reload.

He watched the fleeing figure as he snatched bullets from the loops on his cartridge belt and thumbed them into the cylinder. He saw Ryker stagger and miss a step before going on at a slower pace. Moran jumped up and started in pursuit. Ryker ran towards the back of the barn and disappeared around the corner. But a moment later he came back out of cover and fired two more shots in Moran's direction.

Moran pushed to his feet. He sent a shot at the corner

as the figure disappeared around it again, and ran wide as he headed in the same direction. He reached the corner, flattened against the wall, and risked a glance around it. The back lots were heavily shadowed, but he caught a glimpse of movement ahead and continued the chase.

As he passed a black alley mouth a voice called out to him. Moran halted abruptly, expecting a shot.

'Stand still,' the voice commanded. 'This is Deputy Sheriff Davis. What's with the shooting?'

'I'm Slade Moran, Davis. One of the men involved in the shooting is getting away across the back lots. Come with me. We'll catch him and you can ask him about the shooting. I'd like to hear what he's got to say.'

Davis emerged from the alley. Starlight glinted on the gun he was holding. 'Is it that killer you're after?' he demanded.

'No.' Moran set off again and Davis accompanied him. 'This is a part of your local trouble. Lieutenant Ryker and an army detail were on duty in town, and Ryker set his men on me. They ambushed me in the livery barn, and Ryker got away through a side door. I have a feeling he's heading for Donovan's saloon. Where's the sheriff?'

'I've no idea,' Davis replied. 'It ain't like him to miss out on any shooting. He's always right on the spot.'

A gun flashed from the shadows and Moran heard a slug whine overhead. He and Davis separated, and the deputy sent three shots in reply. Moran flattened against the rear wall of a building fronting the street and continued towards the saloon. Davis rejoined him and they moved forward until, without warning, two guns started shooting at them from the rear of the saloon. They went to ground and stayed low.

'He's got some gun help,' said Davis in an undertone.

'He's gone into the saloon, I reckon,' Moran replied, 'and he's got a couple of Lannick's men to hold us back. Ryker seems to be over-friendly with Lannick.'

'And Lannick is a guy I don't cotton to,' Davis growled. 'I've had an eye on him as a likely trouble-maker for some time. His bunch of hangers-on are little better than riff-raff, but so far I haven't been able to pin anything on them.'

'You might get the chance to change all that before we're through,' Moran observed. 'I've got some men in town; and I must check up on Sergeant Braddock before I go on with this. Braddock was with me in the livery barn, holding off another member of Ryker's detail. I'll fetch him. We may need some help in the saloon.'

'I'll go along with that. And I'd like to know where the sheriff has got to. It just ain't in his nature to miss out on a shoot-up.'

Moran turned to the alley beside the saloon, where the three men of his detail had been left. As he peered into the shadows, Sergeant Braddock's voice called from the street end of the alley.

'Is that you, Captain?'

'Yes, Braddock, I'm looking for the detail,' Moran replied.

'They showed up at the barn when the shooting broke out, sir.' Braddock came along the alley, followed by the three soldiers. 'I have to report that Lieutenant Ryker's men, Mason and Snark fought to a finish, sir. They're both dead. What happened to the lieutenant, Captain?'

'I think he went into the saloon; that's our next job. We have to go in there and check it out.'

When Lieutenant Ryker reached the rear door of the saloon he found it open, and two men with guns in their hands standing in the doorway.

'What's going on, Lieutenant?' one of them demanded.

'Coe, I'm glad to see you.' Ryker holstered his pistol and stepped through the doorway. 'There are a couple of men after me. Hold them off as long as you can to buy me some time. I need to talk to Lannick.'

'Sure. He's up in the office. Go ahead. We'll cover your back.'

Ryker ascended the stairs two at a time and burst into Lannick's office. Lannick looked up from the ledger he was using.

'Now what the hell have you been doing?' Lannick demanded. 'I've heard nothing but shooting for the last fifteen minutes. What did I tell you about laying off for a spell? If you ruin my chances of picking up Doyle then we'll fall out in no uncertain manner.'

'It's that damned army investigator, Moran,' Ryker said angrily. 'He's crowding me, and now he's right outside. I can't go back to the fort because he's already been there, and if I stay here he'll pick me up for sure. I'm gonna have to make a run for it, but fast.'

'You fool!' Lannick sprang to his feet, winced, and pressed both hands to his head. The purple bruise on his left temple where Moran had struck him was seeping blood. His face was pale and he appeared to be on the point of collapsing. 'I've got enough trouble on my plate without you raking up more. If you can't go back to the fort then get the hell out to the CL ranch and lie low there for a few days. That's where I'm heading, anyway. I don't want to see Moran if he's coming here on the war path. Get those saddle-bags out of that corner and help me fill them with the dough from the safe. Jump to it.'

Ryker grabbed up the saddle-bags and held them open while Lannick emptied the contents of the safe into them.

'Is this dough Donovan's?' Ryker demanded.

'The hell it is! Most of it came out of the bank when we robbed it. Get a move on.' Lannick buckled the flaps of the bags as he spoke, and then threw them across his shoulder. 'Let's go into that store cupboard. I've got a bolt-hole in it which leads down into the building next door. No one knows about it. There are a couple of horses in our private barn. We can get out of town before anyone's wise to us.'

Ryker ran to the door in question, jerked it open and entered the big cupboard, which was equipped with shelves and contained the supplies needed to run the saloon. Lannick followed and closed the door behind them. He pointed to the floor, and Ryker saw the outline of a trapdoor.

'Lift that hatch and go down the ladder,' Lannick rapped. 'Make it quick. I'll follow you.'

Ryker wasted no time. He opened the trapdoor and hurriedly descended. Lannick quickly followed him and they soon reached a lower room where a door gave access to the alley on the far side of the saloon. Lannick took the lead through the shadows to the back lots. They moved silently out to an isolated barn, saddled up the two horses inside and led the animals away on foot until they were some considerable distance from the saloon. Then they mounted and rode off into the night, heading for Lannick's ranch. . . .

Moran decided against entering the saloon by the back door and, accompanied by the deputy, Braddock and the detail, led the way along the alley to the street and thence to the batwings. All were holding their pistols.

'Right, let me go first,' Davis said, pushing past Moran. 'I'm the local law here and the townsfolk know it. But be ready to start shooting because Lannick's men won't give up without a fight.'

Davis took a fresh grip on his pistol and burst through the batwings, followed closely by Moran and the soldiers. They fanned out on the threshold of the saloon, their guns covering the dozen or so men at the bar and the tables. The townsmen froze in their actions, shocked by the invasion. They saw military uniforms led by their local representative of the law and remained motionless. Pat Donovan was standing in his usual place behind the bar, and in the silence that followed the appearance of the law party, his voice rang loud and clear across the big room.

'What the hell's going on, Davis? What are you up to? Where's Appleby?'

'That's what I'd like to know,' Davis replied. 'Just stand still, and I'll sort this out. Did Lieutenant Ryker come in here?'

'No,' said Donovan.

'Where's Lannick?' Davis persisted.

'Up in the office, I guess.' Donovan's voice was tinged with impatience. 'That's where he spends his time when he's not gambling. What do you want him for?'

'It's Lieutenant Ryker we want,' Moran cut in, 'and Lannick might know where he is. So where is Lannick?'

'If he ain't in the office then maybe he went out to get his supper,' Donovan suggested. 'If that's so then he'll be back in a little while. Why don't you have a drink while you're waiting?'

The batwings creaked open at Moran's back and he swung round quickly, his gun lifting. The small figure of Doc Harvey appeared.

'Davis,' he said. 'I've been looking everywhere for you. I was called out, and when I went to get my horse out of my barn I found the sheriff there, lying in my gig. You'd better come and take a look. Appleby's dead – shot and killed.'

Silence ensued as the doctor turned and departed. Davis glanced at Moran and then ran to the batwings. A moment later most of the men in the saloon followed him, leaving the batwings swinging slowly in their wake. Moran found himself looking at Pat Donovan, who stood motionless behind the bar, his face expressing shock. Braddock and his detail stood in silence around Moran, awaiting orders.

'Sergeant, take the detail and scout around town for Lieutenant Ryker,' Moran said. 'Try and take him alive if you catch up with him. He's got a lot of explaining to do. Come back to me here when you've checked.'

Braddock saluted and went off with the detail. Moran walked to the bar and gazed intently at Donovan. The saloon owner was composed, his gaze impassive.

'Let's go and check if Lannick is in his office,' Moran suggested. 'It'll save a lot of trouble if I can see him now.'

'You know where the office is,' Donovan replied brusquely. 'You were up there earlier. Lannick won't be pleased to see you after you damn near cracked his skull. He might pull a gun and start shooting, and I don't want to be anywhere around if that happens.'

'Just do like I tell you,' Moran said. 'Make things tough for me and I can return the favour with interest. I have the authority to impose martial law in this town and close this place indefinitely.'

Donovan suppressed a sigh and came out from behind the bar. He led the way to the door at the back of the saloon and pushed it open. Moran followed closely, covering the back door with his pistol. The door was closed, with no sign of any of the hardcases that worked for Lannick. Donovan ascended the stairs to the office, with Moran following closely, and both men strode into the office. Moran saw immediately that the safe had been emptied, and a sigh escaped him. Donovan looked around, nodding, but not immediately noticing the safe.

'He's not here,' he remarked, grinning. 'Like I said, he's probably gone for his supper. It's a regular thing with him about this time of the evening.'

'And does he always take the contents of the safe with him when he leaves the office?' Moran demanded, pointing to the safe. 'That was filled to overflowing with greenbacks.'

Donovan gazed at the safe and his lips moved soundlessly as he cursed under his breath. He shook his head as if he could not believe his eyes.

'Well?' Moran demanded. 'I don't know what it looks like to you but I've got a pretty good idea what's happened.

The trouble Lannick was involved in earlier has spooked him into running, and he's gone, taking the contents of your safe with him.'

'It ain't what it looks like,' Donovan insisted. 'I told Lannick earlier he keeps too much dough in that safe. I reckon he's taken it along to the bank.'

'At this time of the night?' Moran shook his head. 'OK. It's your business, not mine. I'll take a look around town for Lannick, and you'd be well advised to do the same if you want to see the colour of your money again.'

Moran departed quickly, intent on getting to grips with Ryker, leaving Donovan gazing at the empty safe in disbelief.

Lannick and Ryker rode a couple of miles through the night, following a faint trail that led to one of the few horse ranches in the area. Then Ryker suddenly cursed and reined in, Lannick halted and looked at him in surprise.

'Now what in hell's wrong with you?' Lannick demanded.

'I can't pull out now,' Ryker said harshly. 'I ain't running and leaving Cahill on the loose. I'm gonna head back to town and kill that sonofabitch. The court martial should have finished him, but he's coming out on top with that stupid bitch Laura Rivington still hankering after him. Only his death will change her way of thinking.'

'If you take my advice you'll let it go,' Lannick said. 'You can't win that one no matter how you try. But then you never could learn to cut your losses.'

'I'll see Cahill dead before I stop,' Ryker snarled, pulling on his reins and swinging his horse around to face the distant town. 'You go on to the ranch. I'll see you there before sunup, and when I get there I'll be able to rest easy knowing Cahill's dead.'

He set spurs to the flanks of his mount and set off back the way he had come, riding with hatred in his heart and murder on his mind. . . .

Sergeant Braddock organized his detail into two search parties and instructed them.

'We're not out to kill Lieutenant Ryker,' he said. 'What we have to do is locate him and watch his movements until Captain Moran can confront him. Personally, I don't think Ryker will surrender. We all know him only too well, so we'll leave it up to the captain to handle him. Off you go, and play it smart. No sneaking off for a quick drink. If Ryker catches a glimpse of your uniforms he'll start shooting. Let's do this right, and afterwards we can celebrate.'

The two parties of troopers set out to search the town with military thoroughness. Braddock took a trooper with him and checked out the buildings on one side of the street while the other two handled the opposite side. They met at the far end of the street where Braddock took their reports. Ryker had not been sighted.

'I'll report to the captain,' he said. 'Come with me, and stay quiet and alert. We might be able to get a meal now.'

They returned to the saloon and Braddock confronted Donovan, who informed him that Moran had left to talk to Cahill at the guest house. Acting on his initiative, Braddock sent the troopers to the restaurant and went along the street to the guest house where he had seen Cahill. There he found Moran along with Cahill and

Laura Rivington. He made his report and then departed.

Moran sat in the front parlour of the guest house with Cahill and Laura. He had questioned Cahill about the events of the night the money went missing from the Troop office. Cahill struck him as being honest and open, and Moran felt that a miscarriage of justice had occurred at the recent court martial. But he needed to keep an open mind until he had caught Ryker and questioned him, too.

'I think, in view of the incidents occurring this evening, that the verdict of your court martial can be set aside until fresh evidence has been collected for a retrial,' Moran mused. 'There are grounds for serious doubt as to your guilt, and I feel sure Ryker will find himself in a position where his only recourse will be to tell the truth and clear you.'

'Ryker would never do that,' Cahill said, 'if it meant having to admit his guilt.'

'In the meantime, there are one or two lines of inquiry I need to follow up,' Moran said. 'If we can push Ryker into a corner then his only way out will be to admit his guilt. Don't give up hope, whatever you do.'

'I'm feeling happier about the business now we've had this chat, Captain,' Cahill replied. 'I'll remain in town while you carry out your investigation, and I'll be available to talk to you at any hour of the day or the night.'

Moran nodded. 'I should warn you that you could be in considerable danger around town with Ryker on the loose. You'd better take steps to protect yourself, just in case.'

'I'll do that, sir, although I don't think Ryker will make any attempt on my life now the truth is coming out.'

Moran arose. 'I'll see you later. Right now I want to check to see if Ryker is still in town.'

Laura Rivington, who had remained silent during the discussion, got to her feet as Cahill rose, and held out her hand to Moran, who clasped it and shook it firmly.

'You've given us fresh hope, Captain,' she said. 'We'll always be in your debt.'

Moran smiled and turned to depart. He reached the door of the room, and, as he opened it, there came the sound of breaking glass. He swung round to see the window pane, overlooking the street, crashing to the floor. A dark figure was dimly illuminated outside by the lamplight in the room. Moran shouted a quick warning and drew his pistol, but before he could trigger the weapon a gun flashed and thundered from outside. Gun flame lanced through the broken window. Cahill flung up his arms, twisted sharply and fell on his face. Moran hurled himself towards Laura, crashed into her and bundled her to the floor.

He fell heavily, rolled, and came up into the aim. He saw the indistinct figure outside the window turn abruptly and flee, but caught sight of the yellow facings of a cavalry uniform and the metallic glint of the bars of an officer's rank on the shoulders before the man vanished. He got slowly to his feet. The echoes of the shot died away slowly. Moran looked at the inert Cahill and saw blood staining the front of his white shirt. . . .

SEVEN

Moran's ears were ringing from the shooting as he rose, holstered his gun and approached Cahill. He dropped to one knee beside the man, fearing the worst, but was relieved to find that the bullet had struck high in the chest. He looked up as Laura came to his side. Her face was pale, her eyes filled with shock, but she seemed composed and in control of herself.

'He's alive,' Moran rapped. 'Will you fetch the doctor?'

She nodded and hurried from the room. Moran opened Cahill's shirt and saw that the bullet wound was to the right, almost in the shoulder. He heaved a long sigh of relief. Cahill was lucky; if the doctor was any good at his job, he would survive. He ripped open Cahill's shirt and tore it from his limp body to place it against the wound, putting pressure on it to keep it in place. Minutes later, Laura returned, accompanied by Doc Harvey, who took over from Moran.

'I'll need to get him over to my office,' Harvey said sharply. He looked at Moran. 'There'll be some men gathering outside. Get some of them to come in and help carry him across the street.'

Moran went to the street door. Half a dozen townsmen were standing on the boardwalk, and Sergeant Braddock was approaching with the rest of the detail. Moran acquainted Braddock with details of what had happened and the sergeant took his men into the house. They left some minutes later carrying Cahill between them with the doctor fussing around like a broody hen. Moran was about to join Laura Rivington as she hurried over to the doctor's house, but Davis, the deputy sheriff, emerged from the shadows, intercepting him.

'Sheriff Appleby has been murdered,' Davis said in a shocked tone. 'What am I gonna do, Captain?'

'You'll have to step into his boots,' Moran replied sharply. 'Pull yourself together and take control of the situation. Cahill was shot through the window of the guest house. I saw a soldier outside the window, dressed as an officer. Obviously it was Lieutenant Ryker, so you'd better organize a search of the town. Ryker's gone on a killing spree. He could do anything now, and has to be stopped before we find more bodies lying around.'

'Sure,' Davis nodded. 'I'll get on to that right away. But what am I to do about the sheriff? I'll have to look for his killer but I don't know where to start.'

'Ask around and find out where he was last seen. Learn of his last movements and you might come upon his killer. I was involved in the shooting at the stable earlier, before this latest incident, and someone said Appleby had gone to the saloon to talk to Lannick. Check that out and see if it leads anywhere.'

Davis nodded and moved off. Moran waited in front of

the guest house, aware that it would be impossible to locate Ryker until daylight. Braddock returned with the detail, and Moran sent them to search the town again in case Ryker was still around. He thought about the situation for a couple of minutes and then headed for the saloon.

Donovan was still standing behind the bar although the big room was now deserted. A bartender was wiping glasses. Donovan appeared to be in a state of shock, and when he looked up at Moran's approach his eyes seemed unfocused.

'Lannick has obviously run out,' Moran said. 'Have you any idea where he might have gone?'

Donovan shook his head. 'If I knew the answer to that one I'd be riding after him right now,' he replied.

'Sheriff Appleby was murdered this evening. He came in here earlier. Did he see Lannick?'

'I don't know. If he came in, I didn't see him.'

'Do you want Lannick to be picked up by the law?' Moran looked intently into Donovan's eyes, and saw a quick flash of animation in their glassy depths.

'What kind of a question is that?' Donovan demanded. 'My safe has been emptied, and you ask if I want the thief captured?'

'So you're certain that Lannick has run out with your money, huh? You gave evidence at Lieutenant Cahill's court martial. Was he the big gambler he was made out to be?'

'All that came out at the court martial, and I don't see what good it will do to hoe that particular piece of ground again. Read the summary of evidence – it's all in there.'

'I've read the summary, and I'm not happy with some of the statements that were made on oath, particularly yours and Lannick's. I'll give you time to think over what you said, and then we'll have another chat about what really went on.'

'Are you suggesting that I lied on oath?'

'Whatever you did, I'll get at the truth in the end, so bear that in mind.'

Donovan did not reply, and Moran turned to leave, but Donovan called to him as he reached the batwings.

'Listen, I'm in a state of shock right now,' Donovan said heavily. 'I trusted Lannick and he's let me down badly. I don't know how much dough he's run off with until I've checked the books, but it's a fortune, and I'll do anything I can to help the law catch him.'

'That's better,' Moran said. 'I'll see you again tomorrow. The water looks a bit muddy right now, but it'll clear later. Just remember it will be better for us to work together rather than pull in opposite directions.'

Donovan nodded. Moran gazed at him for a moment before departing. He went along the street to the law office, and when he entered he found Davis sitting at the desk, apparently in a state of shock.

'Have you found out anything yet about the sheriff's killer?' Moran asked. Davis nearly jumped out of his seat.

'The hell I have!' The deputy shook his head. 'I don't even know who I should talk to about it. I didn't think Appleby had any enemies. The town has been quiet lately – no trouble to speak of.'

'Until tonight,' Moran amended. 'And you had a bank robbery recently, which should tell you something. Also, there was a robbery at the fort.'

'But that was cleared up. It was proved that Cahill stole that money.'

'All the evidence was circumstantial, and I think it was set up to look like that. But there's a lot of trouble beneath the surface around here. Appleby didn't get to the bottom of it, and now it has got out of hand. Toft and Dawber, the men I shot in the barn, where are they now?'

'They're in the cell.' Davis jerked a thumb towards the big cage at the far end of the office. 'Doc Harvey had them brought over after their wounds were treated. Dawber's still unconscious; Doc's coming to look him over again later. But Toft's wide awake, and he wants to get out of here.'

'Bring him out and I'll talk to him,' Moran said. 'I want to know why he and the others attacked me earlier for no apparent reason.'

Davis got to his feet, picked up the cell key and went to the rear of the office. Moran followed to stand by the door of the big cell. He saw Dawber stretched out on a bunk. Toft was sitting on an adjacent bunk, leaning his uninjured shoulder against the wall. Toft protested vociferously when Davis ordered him to his feet, and cried out in pain when Davis grasped him roughly and dragged him out of the cell. Moran sat down behind the desk as Davis thrust Toft into the seat placed before it.

Toft leaned forward, moaning softly. His face was pale and he seemed to be suffering a great deal of pain. Moran watched him silently for some moments, until Toft looked up at him and grimaced.

'Why can't you leave me alone?' Toft demanded. 'I'm

hurting like hell.'

'I don't doubt that,' Moran observed. 'OK, the sooner we get this over with the better. Tell me what was going on earlier in the saloon. Lannick thought he knew me from somewhere, and he told you and the others to take me out and kill me. So what was he afraid of?'

'I don't know.' Toft put a hand to his injured shoulder and rocked to and fro in pain. 'I only follow orders; I don't give them. Why don't you ask Lannick what it was all about?'

'I can't do that. Lannick has skipped town with all the money that was in Donovan's safe. He probably thought there was big trouble coming so he pulled stakes and ran, leaving the rest of you to carry the can.'

'He's gone?' Toft straightened up and stared at Moran in disbelief. 'No. You're having me on! Lannick has too much to lose around here. He wouldn't run out.'

'Just tell me where he's likely to have gone and I'll haul him back,' Moran said. 'Then we can get to the bottom of this crooked business.'

'I don't know anything.' Toft shook his head. 'I don't even work for Lannick.'

'That's right. You work for Doyle's silver mine. So why were you prepared to commit murder on Lannick's say-so?'

'You're wasting your time,' Toft said. 'I got nothing to say. What do you want me to do, incriminate myself?'

'You'd better think long and hard about your situation,' Moran warned. 'Murder was committed tonight, and someone will hang for that.'

Toft sat up a little straighter. 'Who was killed?' he

demanded. 'You can't pin anything on me.'

'As it happens, I know where you were at that time,' Moran said softly.

'So who the hell got it? Impatience rasped in Toft's voice.

'Appleby,' Davis cut in. He leaned over Toft, seized him roughly by the shoulders and shook him hard. Toft screamed like a woman and fell off the chair when Davis released his hold. 'Come on, open up,' Davis shouted. 'You know more than you're saying. I know you're thick as thieves with Lannick and that bunch at the saloon. Well you won't get away with it any longer. The sheriff closed his eyes to a lot that was going on, but now that's all come to an end and we want the truth. So you'd better open up, Toft. If you don't spill your guts now we'll keep at you until you do.'

'Who killed Appleby?' Toft demanded.

'That's what we're asking you,' Davis replied. He dragged Toft up and thrust him forcefully back on the chair. 'Quit stalling and tell us what's been going on.'

'It's no use asking me.' Toft stifled a groan and shook his head. 'I was on the outside looking in. Lannick's the man you need to talk to.'

'But he ain't around any more,' Davis snarled. 'If you know where he's gone then tell us and we'll pick him up. It sounds like he's the one should carry the can, but if we don't get him then we'll take it out on those he's left behind – and that means you.'

'If you can't find Lannick then pick up Lieutenant Ryker,' Toft said in a low tone. 'Him and Lannick are thicker than molasses.'

'Tell me what you know about Ryker's activities around town,' Moran suggested.

'I don't know what kind of a pull he had on Lannick, but he usually got what he wanted. At times, Lannick bent over backwards to please him.'

'That sounds interesting,' Moran mused. 'Keep talking.'

'I heard it said that Ryker framed Cahill, and Lannick helped him. I know for a fact that Cahill didn't lose the kind of money gambling that they said he did. He played poker, sure, but he didn't go in over his head. Ryker wanted him out of the way, and that was why they framed him.'

Toft slumped then, and would have fallen off the chair if Davis hadn't grabbed and supported him. Moran glanced at Davis.

'You need to get what he said down on paper,' he advised, 'including the part about Ryker, and don't forget to have him sign it.'

'OK,' Davis nodded. 'It'll give me something to do.'

'I'll scout the town again for Ryker.' Moran arose and then paused. 'Make sure you get Toft to include in his statement how he and the others grabbed me to take me out of town and kill me.'

Davis nodded. Moran went to the street door and opened it. He was well pleased with his progress. Toft would talk, and what he had to say could be used as a lever against Lannick. Now, if he could take Ryker he could probably close the case before morning, although he didn't think it would be as easy as that.

*

Sergeant Braddock and his detail paced back and forth along the street, searching for Ryker. They looked in the smaller bars, checked the diner until finally Braddock came to the conclusion that Ryker had left town. He was not surprised by the turn of events. Ryker had really revealed his hand. But Braddock had always been of the opinion that Ryker was bad, and he had never for an instant believed that Cahill was guilty of the charge laid against him.

'Can we get a drink, Sarge?' one of the troopers demanded.

'Not yet,' Braddock replied. 'We'll make completely sure Ryker ain't around before we think of ourselves. I'll report back to the captain and see what else he's got in mind. With any luck we'll be through for the night and then we can knock off duty.'

'The captain's coming along the boardwalk now,' one of the others observed.

Braddock saw the tall figure of Moran approaching and pushed back his shoulders. He saluted when Moran confronted him.

'Any luck, Sergeant?' Moran demanded.

'No, sir. We've been around the street several times but there's no sign of Lieutenant Ryker. I think he's pulled out. There's nowhere he could hide from us. We know all the places where a man might try to conceal himself.'

'I'm sure you're right,' Moran agreed. 'And we can't trail him until sunup, so I think you'd better call it a day. Report to me at the hotel at first light and we'll look for tracks. I think Lannick would have prepared for this kind of problem, so I'm going back to the saloon to talk with Donovan again. I think he knows more about this situation than he's giving out.'

'Very good, sir.' Braddock saluted. 'See you in the morning, Captain.'

Moran nodded and went on to the saloon. There were several townsmen at the bar now, all talking about the sheriff's murder. Donovan was talking vociferously, but fell silent the moment he saw Moran pushing through the batwings. Moran went to the bar.

'I'd like another word with you, Donovan,' Moran said.

'Then you'd better come up to the office,' Donovan replied. He led the way and Moran followed closely.

In the office, Donovan pointed to a seat beside the desk. Moran sat down and Donovan slumped wearily into the chair behind the desk. For a moment there was silence between them. Donovan was agitated, and seemed to be looking everywhere except in Moran's direction. Moran remained silent to make the saloon man squirm even more. In the end it was Donovan who opened the conversation.

'So what's on your mind?' he demanded.

'Lannick and Ryker,' Moran replied.

'Naturally,' Donovan grimaced. 'I can think of no one else at the moment, either. I trusted Lannick with my business and he's robbed me and skipped town. There's nothing I can tell you about him, you know. He was a man of mystery. I don't know where he came from, and I don't know where he's gone.'

'In other words,' Moran said sharply, 'you're not going to tell me anything about him. I guess that tells me a great deal, anyway. Your silence means you're covering for him, so you must be involved in his crooked business. I think you do know where he's gone, Donovan, and I think you're planning to meet up with him later.'

'You're entitled to your opinion.' Donovan shook his head. 'But you're wrong, and one day you'll get the rights of it and know I'm telling the truth.'

Moran got to his feet and departed, loath to waste his time. He went along to the doctor's house, where several townsmen were standing in a crowd outside the front door, evidently awaiting news of the latest shooting. Moran entered the house and found Laura Rivington seated on a chair outside the doctor's office. She looked forlorn and badly shocked, but her face brightened at the sight of the captain.

'How's he doing?' asked Moran as he sat down at her side.

'Doctor Harvey looked out a few minutes ago and told me Richard would live, but he's very badly injured.'

'Look on the bright side,' Moran said, trying to relieve her shock. 'I'm sure he'll pull through OK.'

'Did you get Ryker?' she asked. 'I caught a glimpse of him outside the window of the guest house just as he fired that shot into the room.'

'I saw a man in uniform,' Moran mused, 'but I didn't recognize him.'

'I did,' she said fervently. 'The light fell full on his face as he shot Richard; it was Ryker.'

'And my detail didn't get him.' Moran shook his head. 'However we'll make a full-scale search for him tomorrow. We'll circle the town looking for tracks, and check on every trail we find heading out. We won't give up, and we'll run him down before long. We can chase him much farther than he can run.'

'He must be caught. He won't give up until Richard is dead. I think he's insane.'

'He's a jealous man, and jealousy is the most powerful of all the vices.' Moran looked up as the door to the office opened and Doc Harvey emerged.

'How is he doing, Doc?' Moran asked.

Harvey nodded. His lined face looked grey, but he smiled. 'He'll make it, so long as there are no complications. I've done all I can for the moment. We'll let him rest now and see how he is in the morning. I'll look in on him a couple of times during the night, but I don't expect any problems. He has a strong constitution.'

'I'll stay with him,' Laura said. 'I'll watch him.'

'That's a good idea.' Harvey nodded.

'I'll be around outside the house,' Moran said, and saw Laura's eyes widen and fill with sudden fear.

'Do you expect Ryker to make another attempt on Richard's life?' she demanded.

'No. I'm just being careful,' he replied. 'I'll be on hand in case something does happen, though.'

He took his leave and went back to Donovan's saloon to look for his detail. They were not inside, and, knowing that they would be drinking somewhere, he continued to check the smaller bars until he found them.

'New orders, Sergeant,' Moran said when Braddock straightened and saluted him. 'I've just come from the doctor's house. Cahill is going to pull through. Miss Rivington will sit at his bedside through the night and I think we should mount guard on the house in case Ryker decides to make another attempt on his life.'

107

'That thought was in the back of my mind, Captain.' Braddock glanced at his men. 'We'll cover the front and the back of the house until sunup.'

'I'll leave it in your hands,' Moran said. 'I'll check your guard during the night.'

Braddock saluted, ushered his men out of the bar and marched them away to the doctor's house. Moran heaved a sigh as he stood for a few moments in the shadows on the boardwalk, looking around and listening. The town was quiet now, and he shook his head as he considered the incidents of the evening, wondering what lay behind the actions of some of the townsmen. Lannick was obviously a devious character, for he had fled before events could catch up with him. And who had killed the sheriff? And, more significantly, why had he been murdered?

Moran walked along the street in the dense shadows. There were fewer lamps burning now – miners started work early in the morning, laboured all day and retired early at night. He paused at the door of the law office, hesitated and then entered. Davis was seated at the desk, writing a report of the occurrences of the evening. He looked up at Moran's entrance and put down his pen.

'I've got Toft's statement in black and white,' he said. 'He tried to go back on some of what he said but I made him see sense and he told it like it happened, and he signed it. Dawber's still unconscious so I can't get his statement, but he'll be sitting up and taking notice tomorrow and I'll drag the truth out of him. You should know that I checked the livery barn about half an hour ago and found two soldiers in there, dead. They were with Ryker, shooting at you. Sergeant Braddock said he killed one.'

'And I nailed the other,' said Moran. 'We'll get around to them tomorrow. You're doing a good job. You're a local man, Davis, and have background knowledge that I lack, so tell me a bit about Lannick, and particularly about Lieutenant Ryker. You must have seen him around when he came to town.'

'I sure did. I noticed him because I didn't like him. He had a way about him that made me feel sorry for the soldiers under his command. He was always in Donovan's saloon. He and Lannick were like brothers; you never saw one without the other. Lannick wasn't close to anyone, not even Donovan, but he'd do anything for Ryker, although he wasn't the kind of man to take a shine to anyone.'

'So they had something special going, huh? Ryker was apparently a part of Lannick's set-up, whatever it is. Have you any idea where Lannick might run to now he's pulled out?'

Davis shook his head. 'He's probably fled the county. I wish I could be more help to you, but no one knew much about Lannick.'

'I'll look around the outskirts of the town tomorrow and see if I can pick up tracks.' Moran stifled a yawn and departed. He needed to get a couple of hours' sleep, and there was nothing he could do until sunrise.

He walked to where the sidewalk ended and stared across the intervening space at the black mass of the livery barn. The lantern over the big open doorway was still burning, with only a small radius of brilliance reflecting on the ground beneath it – the surrounding shadows were impenetrable. Moran could understand Ryker's motives; but how had he managed to get ordinary soldiers involved in whatever he was up to? Moran shrugged. It would all come out in the wash, he thought. He turned to retrace his steps to the hotel with the intention of turning in, but the sound of a horse coming into town attracted his attention and he paused to look around.

The shadows on the trail were dense, but movement attracted his eyes and he picked out the shape of a rider moving towards the livery barn. Moran eased back into the shadows. The newcomer was riding at a walk, obviously to limit the noise his horse was making, as if he did not want to attract attention to his arrival. Moran's first thought was that Lannick or Ryker had come back to town. He went forward silently to check on the newcomer.

The man rode through the light cast by the overhead lantern, and, for a moment, Moran could see the horse clearly before it passed on into the stable. It was a black horse, and had two white forelegs. Moran felt a spurt of excitement in his breast when he recalled that Almeyer, the killer he had been trailing, had been riding a horse with similar markings. He saw the rider briefly, and judged him to be of the description he had been given of the man he had pursued until his orders were changed. Moran eased along to the doorway of the barn, flattened against the sun-warped boards and then peered cautiously into the stable. The darkness was only slightly alleviated by the light of the lantern and the interior was still deceptive. Moran waited while the stranger off-saddled his mount and took care of its needs. When the man came towards the front door, carrying his saddle-bags and rifle, Moran eased back into the shadows, drew his pistol from its holster and waited tensely.

The man emerged from the stable, passed Moran and then seemed to sense that he was not alone. He swung quickly, and Moran heard the rasp of steel against leather as the man clawed out his gun.

'I've got you covered,' Moran said sharply. 'Get your hands up.'

He expected the man to freeze, but a hard fist came out of the darkness and crashed against his jaw. The man followed up with his right knee, lifting and slamming it into Moran's groin. Moran dropped his gun and grabbed at the indistinct figure, his left hand finding the barrel of the man's gun as the muzzle lifted to cover him. He thrust the weapon aside, and the next instant he was engaged in a life or death struggle.

EIGHT

Moran sensed that he was bigger and stronger than his unknown adversary, but the man fought like a wildcat. He managed to wrest the pistol from the man's hand, but took a solid punch in the stomach and then a hard chop to the left side of his neck. A saddle-bag hit him in the face, and then the man was swarming all over him, fists coming in from all angles, slamming into his face and his stomach; a knee lifted solidly again to crash into his groin, but he avoided much of the blow by sliding to his left. He struck back quickly, pulling in his chin and lifting his shoulders in defence. He slammed his head forward in a vicious butt and felt the man's nose crunch under the impact. The man eased back then, dropping his saddle-bags and shaking his head before redoubling his efforts. But Moran began to outpunch him, and the man instantly half-turned in an attempt to flee.

Blood was running down Moran's face from a split eyebrow. He blinked furiously as his vision was curtailed. He grasped the man's shoulder with his left hand, swung him round, and loosed a powerful right-hand punch that jerked the man's head back. Moran followed up with his right knee, slamming it into the man's groin. He heard a grunt, a quick intake of breath and then threw a left-hand punch that cracked against the man's jaw. The man lifted his right shoulder as he reached towards his belt, and Moran sensed that he was pulling a knife or another gun. He threw both his arms around the man, pinning his elbows to his sides, and lifted him bodily and slammed him against the wall of the barn. Boards creaked in protest.

Moran threw a succession of heavy punches with his left fist while holding the man still with his right hand clenched in the front of his shirt. The man struggled, but suddenly relaxed and fell inert against Moran, who pushed him to the ground and followed him down, his left fist cocked in case he was shamming. A quick check showed him the man had lost consciousness, and Moran felt around for his pistol. He found it, snatched it up and then got up on one knee and covered his prisoner.

Had he finally caught up with Almeyer? The killer's tracks had disappeared ten miles out of town, and it was likely that Almeyer had waited around for darkness before venturing into the community. Moran recalled the description he had been given of the killer. It was not enough to enable him to identify the man, but would be sufficient to hold him until his identity could be checked.

The man groaned and stiffened. Moran stuck the muzzle of his pistol against his neck.

'Get to your feet and stand still,' he ordered. 'Give me any more trouble and you'll collect a slug.'

'Who are you – a lawman? What's the big idea attacking me?'

'As I recall, you attacked me. So who are you and what's your business?'

'I don't have to tell you anything. I rode into town peaceable and you were waiting for me. I hit you because I thought you were gonna roll me for my dough. So who are you, and why were you hiding in the shadows?'

'You don't sound like an honest man,' Moran mused. 'What do you call yourself?'

'Ben Buttifant. I've come to town on business for my boss.'

'And who's your boss?'

'That's my business.'

'I suspect you of being a deserter from the army, name of Almeyer, who is accused of killing an officer. You fit the description I have, and you're riding a black horse with two white forelegs. The killer is said to have one similarly marked. So I'm gonna hold you for questioning.'

'You can't hold me against my will,' Buttifant said.

'Consider yourself under arrest. On your feet and pick up your saddle-bags. Walk ahead of me along the street to the law office. I'm putting you behind bars until I'm satisfied about your identity.'

Buttifant got up, collected his saddle-bags, and set off along the street, protesting vociferously. Moran followed him closely, his pistol cocked. They were passing Donovan's saloon when the batwings creaked open and Sergeant Braddock emerged. Lamplight issuing from an adjacent window streamed across the boardwalk, enabling Braddock to see Moran and his prisoner.

'Captain, what's going on?' Braddock demanded.

'This man just rode into town on a horse like the one

the killer I was chasing was supposed to be using, and he has the same build as Almeyer.'

'Let me take a look at him, sir.' Braddock approached Buttifant, turned him to face the light from a window. 'I thought he looked familiar, Captain,' he said. 'This ain't your killer, sir; he's Mack Jennings, one of our deserters from the fort.'

'That's interesting,' Moran observed. 'How long has he been a deserter?'

'About four months, as I remember, sir.'

'Just my luck to run into you, Braddock,' Jennings growled. 'What are you doing in town? I thought this place was off limits to soldiers.'

'Have you seen Lieutenant Ryker around?' Moran demanded.

'Ryker!' Jennings spat on the ground. 'I deserted to get away from that buzzard.'

'Let's go to the jail and get some questions and answers going,' Moran said. 'Stay with me, Braddock. You should be able to help with some of the questions I need to ask.'

They entered the law office, and Moran got his first good look at the prisoner. He wondered about the set-up Jennings was in. It was unusual for a military deserter to remain in proximity to the fort from which he deserted, for his only salvation was in gaining distance from the post where he served.

Braddock pushed Jennings into a seat and stood behind him. Davis emerged from a room to the left of the big cage, and gazed at Jennings with interest.

'Where did you pick him up?' he demanded.

'Do you know him?' Moran asked.

'Sure. He was a trouble-maker around town until he deserted. I thought he'd be miles away by now. He used to hang around Donovan's saloon with several soldiers; they're the men who gave all soldiers a bad name around here.'

'Can you name any of the others he hung around with?' Moran said.

'There was a certain bunch, always picking fights with townsmen and causing a nuisance.' Davis frowned as he considered. 'Yeah, I recall them – Jennings, Borden, Teasdale and Farrell. What happened to your sidekicks, Jennings? They went missing around town the same time you faded out.'

'I'll tell you about them,' said Braddock, 'they all deserted. So where are they, Jennings? Are they still hanging around with you?'

'We went our separate ways when we ditched the army,' replied Jennings sullenly. 'I ain't seen any of them since we quit.'

'Then they have more sense than you,' Braddock opined. 'Why did you stick around? You might have known you stood a good chance of being recognized. Was a woman involved?'

'I don't have to give you my reasons.'

'You will, one way or another,' Braddock retorted. 'And address me as Sergeant when you talk to me. You're in for a lot of grief when we get you back to the fort, Jennings.'

'Were you mixed up in the bank robbery we had here recently?' Davis asked. 'A witness said he thought he recognized a couple of the robbers as being soldiers from the fort. He couldn't identify them because they were out of

116

uniform and seemed different to how they looked normally.'

Jennings didn't reply and Moran took over the questioning. But Jennings remained silent about his recent whereabouts.

'Put him in the cell, Sergeant,' Moran said when his patience was exhausted. 'We'll send him back to the fort in the morning.'

Moran took his leave then, and headed for the hotel with the intention of turning in for a couple of hours. . . .

After he left Grey Ridge, Lannick pushed his horse as fast as he dared through the night. There was a trail of sorts leading to the CL ranch, which he owned in partnership with a man named Tom Chivers. He was thoughtful as he rode, undecided about his future in the county. Killing Sheriff Appleby had thrown his plans into chaos, and he rued the murder although he knew Appleby had exceeded his usefulness. But he needed to pull off the robbery of silver from Doyle's mine, and when that had been accomplished successfully he would be better able to assess the situation and make a firm decision about pulling out permanently. In any case, he could not return to town, having stolen Donovan's cash, and he sensed that a complete change of scenery would be the safest way to solve his problems.

He was disappointed in his half-brother. Ryker had seemed to be right to play a big part in his plans, but was lacking in what it took to make a successful career in big crime. Lannick was aware that he had to come to a decision about Ryker. A bullet in the back was a good remedy;

the thought of killing a blood relation did not bother Lannick one whit.

He pulled his horse down to a walk when he neared the ranch, still undecided about his future. It all depended on what Ryker did back in town. If he killed Cahill and got away with it then all well and good, but he had niggling doubts about Ryker's ability to succeed. He pushed the matter to the back of his mind, aware that he had a little time in which to think over his plans. He rode into the ranch yard, crossed to the small house and dismounted, taking his saddle-bags with him when he entered the building.

Tom Chivers was seated at a desk in a corner of the living room, writing in a ledger. He was tall and broad-shouldered, looked old at forty-two. His hair was sparse and grey; his eyes a washed-out blue. His hands trembled as he totted up figures, and sweat beaded his forehead. He looked up at Lannick, and started in surprise at the sight of his partner.

'I wasn't expecting you to show up today,' Chivers said. 'Is anything wrong in town?'

'Nothing I can't handle.' Lannick dumped his saddle-bags on the desk. 'Take a look at what I got here, Tom, and then try and make me believe that crime doesn't pay.' He opened the bags and tipped their contents on the desk. 'Count that little lot and see what you come up with.'

'Say, have you robbed the bank again?' Chivers demanded.

'I cleaned out Donovan's safe,' Lannick grinned. 'Most of it was mine, anyway.'

'Donovan will be madder than a wet hen. You wanta be

118

careful with him. He could make bad trouble for us.'

'What's he gonna do, complain to the local law that I stole his share of the bank robbery?' Lannick laughed. 'He ain't gonna do a blamed thing. I made him a lot of dough over the past year.'

'Which he put in the bank, then lost in the robbery.' Chivers leaned back in his seat. 'One of these days I reckon you're gonna get just too clever.'

'Is that so? I got some news for you, Tom. Appleby was killed in town tonight.'

'Who in hell did that?' Chivers gasped.

'I did. He's been stepping out of line for some time now, and tonight he went just a bit too far. But there's some more serious news you can pass on to your deserter pards. A stranger showed up in the saloon earlier today, and it turned out he's an army man – Captain Moran of the Special Investigation Department. I heard he was trailing an army killer, but he could be after the deserters you've got hanging around here so tell them to lie low for a spell, or pull out until the heat's off.'

'That ain't so good,' Chivers mused. 'I sent one of them, Jennings, into town earlier.'

'Let's hope he doesn't run into that investigator – he's one smart galoot. I set three men on him and he killed one and downed the other two. Ryker had some soldiers in town with him on a work detail and they tried for Moran but came off second best.

'Me and Ryker left town together on the run, but Ryker went back to kill Cahill, that officer he got court martialled.'

'That doesn't sound so good.' Chivers shook his head.

'But there's nothing around the ranch to interest an army investigator except the deserters. I'll have them ride out to the line camp on Silver Creek first thing in the morning. That should take care of it. You'll have to lie low, Lannick, especially if they figure you killed Appleby.'

'Ryker's the one I'm worried about,' Lannick mused. 'He's got a bee in his bonnet about the Rivington gal, and she won't have anything to do with him. He could turn real nasty over her. I saw it in his eyes today.'

'He's your brother, ain't he?'

'Half-brother.'

'That could make things tough if he causes trouble.'

'No it won't. I'll kill him if he starts along that trail. Say, I've had a rough time this evening. I'll turn in, and we'll see what the situation looks like in the morning.'

'What are you gonna do with this dough?'

'You can put it in your safe.' Lannick shrugged.

'Not me. If an army long-nose is doing the rounds then I don't want it on the place.'

'OK, I'll take care of it in the morning. Stick it in your safe until tomorrow.' Lannick turned away and went to the room he used when staying at the ranch.

When Ryker hurried away from the guest house he was certain he had killed Richard Cahill. In the split second of the shooting he saw Cahill fall with blood on his chest, and he was exhilarated as he hunted cover in the shadows. He ran into an alley and made for the back lots where he had left his horse. Moments later he was riding into the night, making for the CL horse ranch, but he covered no more than a mile before reining in and stepping down from his saddle. He looked back towards the town, saw the dim light of a couple of lanterns seemingly beckoning him, and realized he still had another job to do.

That army investigator, Moran, was a tough nut, and had to be put away before he could get to grips with the local situation. It should be easy to ambush him. He considered for a moment, aware that his career as an officer was as good as over, but if Moran caught him he would likely be charged with murder, so he had to get in first and kill the long-nose. He turned his horse and rode back to town, heading for the rear of the hotel, where he dismounted and tethered his horse to a tree in dense shadow. His fingers were trembling with suppressed excitement as he checked his gun. Moran had to be killed before he could report on the events of the evening.

He entered the alley beside the hotel and walked to the street end, pausing at a side window to peer into the lobby. A woman was behind the reception desk. Ryker continued on to the street. He needed to know if Moran was in the hotel. He peered around in the dark. There was little activity now the excitement of the shooting had died down. He went to the front door of the hotel and entered. It would be tough luck if Moran happened to appear right now, and he kept his hand close to the butt of his pistol as he walked to the desk.

'Lieutenant Ryker!' exclaimed the receptionist, a tall, slender woman in her thirties. She was good looking, her smile attractive. 'I thought the town was off limits to soldiers!'

'Hello, Myra,' he replied. 'I'm on duty. Captain Moran is booked in here for tonight. I'm to escort him out to the fort in the morning. Is he in his room, do you know?'

She glanced in the hotel register for Moran's room number, and then checked the key board on the back wall. 'His key is here so he must still be out. Shall I tell him you called? I'll be on duty until midnight.'

'Say nothing, please,' he responded. 'If he knows I'm here he may want me to take him out to the fort tonight. I'll drop in on him unannounced in the morning.'

He left the hotel, sought the cover of the alley and stood in complete darkness, watching the street for Moran's approach. He had barely settled himself when he heard footsteps approaching on the sidewalk. He moved deeper into the alley and drew his gun. A moment later three men passed the alley mouth, two of them in uniform. He recognized the big figure of Sergeant Braddock, saw the other was Moran and finally recognized Jennings, the deserter who had been hiding out at the CL ranch.

Ryker remained in cover, watching the trio, and, when they entered the law office, he holstered his gun and moved in close. He risked a look through the front window and saw Jennings seated on a chair in front of the desk with Braddock standing behind him. So Jennings was under arrest. He considered the implications. If Jennings told his captors where he had been hiding then the other deserters at the CL ranch would be in jeopardy – a troop of cavalry would head out to the ranch and clean them out.

For some moments Ryker was undecided. Should he shoot Jennings to prevent him talking, or wait to see what developed? He held his fire and waited, and when

Jennings was thrust into the cage at the far end of the office and locked in, it seemed that he had made the right decision. When Moran turned to leave, Ryker ran into the alley beside the law office. As the captain passed the alley mouth, Ryker lunged at him from the shadows and struck viciously with his pistol. The blow crashed against Moran's right temple with a solid thud and he folded without a sound. Ryker grasped him by the shoulders and dragged him into the alley.

For several tense moments Ryker stood poised over Moran, intending to shoot him, but a doubt entered his mind and he stayed his hand, thinking it might be better to take Moran out to the ranch and hand him over to Lannick. He considered his options, and decided that taking Moran out of town would be the right thing to do. He holstered his gun and pulled Moran into a sitting position.

Moran's chin was on his chest. He was not wholly unconscious, aware only of pain in his head, but the deep blackness of unconscious was hovering above the limit of his awareness like a buzzard preparing to attack its prey. When Ryker heaved him upright the movement cleared some of the shadows from his brain, but he gave no indication of returning to consciousness. He sagged against Ryker, letting the man take his whole weight. He was aware of being dragged along the alley towards the back lots, but had not the strength to fight back.

When Ryker reached his waiting horse he hefted Moran up across the saddle and led the animal to the rear of the livery barn. Moran returned to normal with each passing moment, but still gave no sign of his improving condition. When Ryker bent over him to check his degree of unconsciousness, Moran grasped him by the right shoulder with his left hand and struck out with his clenched right fist. His knuckles smacked against Ryker's jaw, and he retained his hold as Ryker's knees buckled. Ryker dropped to the ground and Moran went with him, over the back of the horse.

When they hit the ground, Moran was atop Ryker, and struck several heavy blows at his face. Ryker made no attempt to fight back. He grabbed for the butt of his pistol and dragged it clear of its holster. Moran heard the rasp of the weapon pulling clear of leather and realized his danger. He grasped Ryker's gun wrist, forced the muzzle of the gun away from his body, and exerted pressure on the wrist. The gun exploded in flame and thunder. Moran struck again with his right fist and Ryker slumped inertly.

Moran got unsteadily to his feet. Pain was throbbing through his right temple and down the right side of his neck as far as his shoulder blade. When he bent to scrabble for Ryker's gun he almost overbalanced and fell, but his searching fingers found the butt of the weapon and he snatched it up. Only then did he peer at Ryker's face to check the identity of his attacker. He leaned against the waiting horse and waited for the renegade officer to regain his senses.

Ryker opened his eyes at last and looked up to see the black shape of Moran standing over him. He could not see the gun in Moran's hand but had no doubt that he was being menaced with a weapon.

'You've been real busy this evening,' Moran observed. 'Get up and we'll go along to the law office. I'll be interested to know what's on your mind.'

Ryker got slowly to his feet. Moran cocked his gun and Ryker turned to head for the law office. They went by way of the main street, Moran ready for anything Ryker might try; equally, Ryker was aware that Moran was not going to be caught out again. They reached the law office without incident. Ryker opened the door and entered.

Davis got up from his desk, grinning when he saw Ryker.

'You got him,' he said gleefully. 'Where was he skulking? Did you kill the sheriff, Ryker?'

'Don't try to pin that on me,' Ryker retorted.

'You're in deep trouble without the sheriff's death on your hands,' Moran observed. 'Just tell me where Lannick is.'

'How should I know? I'm not his keeper.'

'So why did you attack me this evening?' Moran demanded.

'Who said I did?' Ryker smiled. 'You might have a big chore proving that, Captain. I don't think you can prove anything, come to that. You've haven't got enough to hold me.'

'You shot Cahill,' Moran said, nodding. 'I saw you at the guest house window, and Laura Rivington recognized you, too. That's enough to hold you, and by the time I get through checking you out I expect there'll be a number of other charges to be brought against you.'

Ryker scowled and clamped his teeth together. Moran, watching him closely, heaved a sigh and motioned to Davis.

'Put him behind bars,' he said. 'He'll go to the fort in the morning with Jennings.'

'I could get the truth out of him,' Davis said, clenching his hands. 'And I wanta know who killed the sheriff.'

'Not now.' Moran shook his head. 'Let him sleep on it tonight. In the morning he might see things differently. Put him behind bars.'

Ryker was locked in the cage. When Davis returned to his desk, Moran set off for the hotel in the hope of getting a well-earned rest. He was only half alert as he went along the boardwalk, looking into the surrounding shadows, his right hand close to the butt of his holstered pistol, and he was faintly surprised when he reached the hotel lobby without incident. But his eyes narrowed when he saw the smart figure of Pat Donovan standing by the reception desk. He went forward slowly, wondering what more had cropped up.

Donovan came forward when he saw Moran. His face was gaunt, showed exhaustion and despair. He showed his empty palms to Moran as they met in the centre of the lobby, and then let his shoulders slump and his breath escape in a long sigh.

'I've thought over the situation,' Donovan said, 'and the conclusion I've reached is that there is nothing to think over. My only chance of coming out of this business with any kind of a profit is to tell you where you can find Lannick and hope that you can pick him up.'

'I thought you might have second thoughts about your position,' Moran said. 'If you are ready to tell me about Lannick then come along to the law office and we'll talk.'

Donovan sighed again, shaking his head as he considered and finally nodded. 'I'm ready to talk so long as you don't use what I tell you against me.'

'I can't promise you that.' Moran shook his head. 'I work for the military, and have authority only in military matters. Everything else comes under the jurisdiction of the local law, and they'll have to be in on this every step of the way. What happens to you will depend on the deputy, Davis.'

Donovan moistened his lips. He nodded. 'OK,' he said grudgingly. 'Have it your way. At best I'm hoping to get my dough back, but if that is not possible then I certainly want to see Lannick pay for what he's done.'

'So come and tell me what you know,' Moran said, 'and then we'll see what can be done. I can't make any promises, and all I'm really interested in at this moment are the soldiers who deserted from the fort.'

'You'll get them,' Donovan said grimly, 'and a lot more beside.'

Moran put a hand on Donovan's arm, drew him to the street door and together they went along to the law office.

NINE

Donovan sat before the desk in the law office, brooding over his situation while Moran told Deputy Sheriff Davis of Lannick's defection with Donovan's money. Davis turned on Donovan immediately.

'Why didn't you report this to me when it happened?' he demanded.

'I didn't know for certain that Lannick had gone for good,' Donovan replied.

'So why are you telling me now?' Davis insisted. 'What's happened since Lannick ran out?'

'I just know he's gone for good.' Donovan shrugged his shoulders.

'Where is Lannick?' Moran cut in. He made a sharp motion with his right hand when Davis opened his mouth to continue bullying Donovan and Davis remained silent.

'Lannick owns half the CL ranch and I reckon that's where he's gone,' said Donovan. 'If you ride out there before sunup you might grab him before he pulls out for other parts.'

'And you say he stole your money.' Davis dropped a

hand to the butt of his gun. 'How much was in your safe?'

'At least six thousand dollars, I guess.'

'Why in hell didn't you put that kind of dough in the bank?' Davis demanded. 'You were asking for trouble, keeping it in your office.'

'If I'd played safe and banked it I would have lost it when the bank was robbed,' Donovan replied.

'I'll get a posse and ride out to the CL.' Davis looked questioningly at Moran. 'Will you ride with us?'

'This has nothing to do with the army,' Moran observed. 'My authority is to round up the deserters from the fort.'

'There are several army deserters out at the CL,' said Donovan. 'Lannick had an arrangement with Ryker. They sent deserters out to work the ranch.'

'So that's why they've never been caught.' Davis shook his head. 'They've been hiding out there all the time.' He turned on his heel and walked to the door of the big cell. 'Hey, Jennings,' he called. 'Is that where you've been hiding out – you and the other deserters? Have you been working as horse wranglers for Lannick?'

Jennings did not reply.

'Get your posse together,' Moran said briskly. 'I'll get my detail to ride with us. With any luck we can catch those deserters on the hop and finish the whole business before dawn. We'll be at the stable ready to ride in thirty minutes.'

'Have you finished with me now?' Donovan asked. 'I got things to do.'

'Sure.' Davis nodded. 'I'll talk to you again in the morning. Don't leave town.'

Donovan departed hurriedly. Moran left the jail and crossed the street to the doctor's house. As he approached the front door a low voice challenged him from the surrounding shadows and he answered quickly.

'I'm Captain Moran.'

A figure eased around the front corner of the house and came forward, gun in hand.

'Sergeant Braddock is inside the house with Miss Rivington, sir,' the soldier reported. 'Shall I call him?'

'I'll find him,' Moran said, and approached the front door.

The door was opened almost immediately when Moran rapped on it and Sergeant Braddock emerged. He saluted.

'Everything's under control, Captain,' Braddock reported.

Moran acquainted the sergeant with the latest development, and then said, 'We'll ride with the posse and take the deserters. With Ryker in jail there's no threat to Richard Cahill so we can leave him safely in the doctor's care. The posse will ride out in thirty minutes. Have the men ready to ride by then, and saddle my horse. 'I'll see you at the livery barn.'

'Yes, sir!' Braddock saluted and called to his men.

Moran went into the house to speak to Laura Rivington. He found her sitting by Cahill's bed in a small room beyond the doctor's office. Cahill was sleeping peacefully.

'Is anything wrong, Captain?' Laura demanded.

He told her of Ryker's arrest, and said, 'With Ryker in jail there's no longer a threat to Richard. I'm taking my men away now. We have a chore to handle out of town and should be back early tomorrow morning. I'll come and talk to you again when I return.'

She thanked him profusely and he departed.

Donovan did not return to the saloon when he left the law office. He headed for the shacks at the end of the street, picked his way through the muddle of little buildings and knocked on the door of a cabin that stood slightly apart from the rest. The door was opened by a great bear of a man with thick, powerful arms and a moon face that had a fleshy, squashed look.

'Mr Donovan, what brings you here at this time of night?' the man growled.

'I want you to do a chore for me, Henty,' Donovan replied. 'Ride out to the CL ranch and tell Lannick or Chivers that a posse is coming out there to pick up Lannick and the deserters. Can you do that, and beat the posse there?'

'Sure thing, Mr Donovan, I'm on my way.' Chuck Henty pushed past Donovan and hurried around to the back of the cabin.

A few moments later, when the sound of receding hoofs reached Donovan, he smiled and made his way back to the saloon. . . .

Moran went to the hotel room to collect his rifle and saddle-bags before going on to the livery barn. There was a great deal of activity there. Half a dozen townsmen had been summoned to form a posse and they were saddling up and preparing to ride, chattering excitedly at the prospect of action against wrong-doers. Deputy Sheriff Davis was the centre of attention. He was keenly aware of his new position in the community. With Sheriff Appleby dead, Davis was running things, and he wanted to make a good job of his first action as leader of the local law department.

'We're heading out to the CL ranch,' Davis explained when the posse was finally ready to ride. 'Nick Lannick should be out there and he is wanted by the law.'

'What's he done?' someone demanded.

Davis ignored the question. 'I have information that some army deserters are holed up at the ranch, and we're gonna bring them back to the army. Captain Moran and a military detail are riding with us, and they'll take charge of the deserters. Let's do a good job, huh?'

There was a chorus of assent as the posse men led their horses out of the barn. They swung into their saddles, fell in behind Davis, Moran and the military detail and left town at a canter, riding in pairs. There was light enough to see the trail leading to the CL ranch. A half moon was suspended in the sky above a distant peak, shining like a great celestial lantern. Countless stars were sprinkled across the black sky, twinkling remotely and a strong breeze blew into their faces during the eight mile ride.

The CL ranch was in darkness when Chuck Henty reached it. He galloped across the yard and hauled on his reins to bring his lathered horse to a sliding halt beside the porch. He slid out of the saddle, crossed the porch and hammered on the front door with the butt of his pistol. The sounds echoed across the yard and, when no apparent reaction came from within the building, Henty added his voice to the clamour.

A light came on in the front upper room, a window was

opened noisily and then a voice called from the window.

'Who in hell is making that racket? Chivers demanded. 'Is the barn on fire?'

Henty stepped off the porch and looked up at the window. He shouted his message, turned and climbed back into his saddle, and rode away quickly.

Chivers shook off his weariness as he digested the information, and then ran to Lannick's room. Lannick was in the act of putting a match to the lamp beside his bed. He cursed at the news and sprang up to dress feverishly.

'Go saddle my horse, Tom,' he rapped, 'and tell any deserters on the place to pull out fast. I'll head back to town – they won't think of looking for me there. Don't stand with your mouth open. That posse will be riding in here any minute now.'

'Henty said Donovan sent the warning,' Chivers said. 'And you stole his money?'

'Don't let that fool you.' Lannick grinned. 'Donovan's after a slice of the silver shipment, so we'll take advantage of his greed and use him as I see fit. Now get my horse saddled up and roust out the deserters. Get them moving to the line camp. When the posse shows up all you've got to do is act dumb. You ain't seen me in weeks and there ain't any deserters on this spread.'

Chivers dashed off to the bunk house and then the corral. Lannick dressed for the trail in record time, grabbed his saddle-bags from the safe in the office and ran across to the corral. He was galloping back to town by a circuitous route when the drumming hoofs of a large mounted party sounded in the distance, approaching the ranch.

The posse reined up far enough out from the darkened ranch for their approach to be unheard by the occupants. Davis split the men into four small groups before sending them in to surround the place. His final instructions were concise and clear.

'No shooting unless you're fired at,' he said, 'and before you shoot you must declare yourselves as posse men. I don't think the deserters will surrender. They'll go down fighting, so be ready for action. Get into position silently so they don't know we are around until we're ready for them. OK, let's go get 'em.'

Moran and his military detail rode together, and Moran led the way around the back of the ranch house to the bunk house near the big corral. A dozen or more horses were in the corral, and they began to get excited when the soldiers drew near. Braddock was at Moran's side, and Moran leaned towards him and spoke in an undertone.

'Any deserters hiding out here will be in the bunk house, I'm thinking,' he said. 'Surround the place and then we'll start them up. Leave the talking to me, but be ready to cut loose at them at the first sign of resistance.'

'Sure thing, Captain.' Braddock relayed the orders to his men. They dismounted, drew their weapons and prepared to fight.

Moran sat his horse in front of the bunk house. Silence hung over the spread. He waited until he heard Davis shouting at the front of the ranch house, issuing an ultimatum. When the deputy fell silent a shot sounded, blasting out the silence and sending a string of echoes rolling away through the still night. Moran drew his pistol, cocked it and gave notice of his presence.

'Hello, the bunk house,' he called. 'Come on out with your hands up. This is a lawful posse out here. The place is surrounded and we want to do this without shooting.'

Silence followed his words. Nothing moved inside the bunk house. Moran watched the window beside the door of the building. He caught a slight movement when a face was pressed close to the glass and then withdrawn quickly. Nothing happened for several tense moments until, suddenly, glass shattered as the window was broken by a gun barrel. The next instant a string of shots came hammering from the bunk house, aimed in Moran's direction, but he was already out of his saddle and crouching on one knee. His horse cantered away to the right, out of the line of fire.

Moran lifted his pistol and sent two shots at the window, aiming for muzzle flame. He dropped flat as slugs crackled around him, and kept firing, aiming his shots with great care. Braddock and his men were close to the front wall of the bunk house, covering the door, and Moran saw the sergeant's big figure sneaking along the wall towards the window.

Braddock reached the side of the window, leaned forward and thrust his gun hand in through the aperture. He triggered the weapon twice in quick succession, and the gun that had been firing at Moran fell silent. Braddock moved back several feet but kept his pistol trained on the window. Moran called again.

'You in the bunk house, there's no escape. Throw down your guns and come out the door with your hands up. You don't have a choice. We've got the place sewed up tight. Give up now and save bloodshed.'

'Go to hell!' a voice replied from the darkness within

135

the building. 'You'll never take us alive. If you want us then come and get us.'

Two pistols began shooting fast through the window. Moran ducked and returned fire. He had hoped to avoid a violent confrontation, but it was his experience that cornered deserters would rather die fighting than surrender. He could hear a voice shouting inside the bunk house but could not make out what was being said. Then the shooting abated slowly and silence fell again.

'Hey, you out there; did you say you're with a posse?'

'That's right,' Moran replied. 'Are you coming out peaceably?'

'Sure we are. Why would we wanta fight with the law?'

'OK, put down your guns and come out with your hands up.'

The door of the bunk house opened slowly. Braddock and the soldiers moved around the outside in a half circle, guns covering the doorway. A man in shirt sleeves and no boots appeared in the doorway with his hands shoulder high. He paused and looked around.

'Come on out and keep your hands up where we can see them,' Moran called. 'Do as you're told and no one will get hurt.'

Seven men filed out of the bunk house, all with their hands up. Braddock and his men searched them quickly and efficiently.

'They're clean, Captain,' Braddock reported.

'Get a lamp and let's take a look at them,' Moran said.

'What's this all about?' demanded a big man at the front of the group. 'I'm the ramrod here. That fool Bill Fenton opened up at you, and he's lying dead inside.

136

What's the idea showing up here at this time of the night and throwing a scare into us? We reckoned you were horse thieves. That's why we started shooting. What's going on?'

'Just give us a couple of minutes,' Moran replied.

Braddock emerged from the bunk house carrying a lantern. The yellow light danced uncertainly and cast deceptive shadows. The sergeant walked along the line of men, holding the lantern shoulder high, examining each face intently. When he reached the end of the line he turned to Moran.

'There ain't a deserter among them that I know of, Captain,' he reported.

'Of course there ain't,' growled the ramrod. 'We wouldn't employ their like if we were dying for help. We sell a lot of remounts to the local cavalry, so how far do you think we'd get if half our crew were army deserters? You better go over to the house and talk to the boss. He'll set you straight.'

Moran looked in the direction of the house. Lights were shining in the front windows. There had been no shooting after the initial shot.

'Stay with these men for the moment. Sergeant,' Moran said. 'I'll go check with Davis.'

He fetched his horse, swung into the saddle and rode across to the house. Posse men were standing around the porch with guns levelled. A big man was talking angrily to the stolid deputy, Davis.

'So what's going on, Chivers?' Davis said as Moran joined them. 'I got a report that Lannick is out here, and you're employing deserters from the fort.' He paused and turned his attention to Moran. 'What happened at the bunk house, Captain? We heard shooting.'

'There are no deserters,' Moran replied. 'A man named Bill Fenton, thinking we were horse thieves, started shooting and was killed in the exchange of shots.'

Chivers cursed at the news and rounded angrily on Davis. 'Just what the hell are you playing at, Davis?' he demanded. 'Where's Sheriff Appleby? He would have handled this differently. You've got no right coming in here and shooting up the place.'

'Is Lannick here?' Moran demanded.

'The hell he is!' Chivers snarled. 'I ain't seen him in a coon's age.'

'Have you searched the house?' Moran asked Davis.

'A couple of men are doing that right now,' Davis said heavily. 'And don't tell me how to do my job, Chivers. I'll do what I have to according to the needs of the law, and don't you forget it. I'm not satisfied with this. I was told Lannick would be here and you say he ain't. If I find him hiding on the spread I'll throw the book at you.'

'Look all you want,' Chivers said angrily. 'I'm going back to bed. I've got work to do in the morning, with an early start. Shut the gate when you leave, huh?'

Lannick reached town around midnight and dismounted at the rear of the saloon. He could see a light in the upstairs office, which overlooked the back lots, and he grinned as he imagined Donovan's thoughts on his missing money. Lannick had stolen it with no intention of returning it, but his plans were fluid and he was prepared to return Donovan's cash in the interests of better things to come.

He unlocked the back door to the saloon, entered and ascended the stairs to the office. Donovan sat at the desk, going through some ledgers, and Lannick laughed at the expression which crossed the bar owner's face when he looked up.

'You stole my dough!' Donovan accused. He opened his right-hand drawer and his hand hovered over a pistol inside.

'Don't lift that gun,' Lannick warned. 'I took the money because I expected the law to come calling when Appleby's body was found, and if they saw your dough in the safe they would know some of it came from the bank robbery – wads of new notes still with bank wrappers on them.' He tossed the bulging saddle-bags on the desk. 'Here you are, and don't bother to count it. Who told the law I was out at CL? Davis showed up there with a posse, hunting me and the army deserters. Did you tell him about my setup?'

'What did you expect? I thought you ran out with my dough and I wanted it back. But I sent Chuck Henty out to the ranch to warn you and Chivers that the posse was on its way.'

'That's something in your favour, anyway,' Lannick admitted grudgingly. 'Now you can do something else. I want Toft out of jail. We're not gonna wait until Doyle ships his silver to the bank; we're going up to the mine now to take it before we all skedaddle.'

'I can't leave,' Donovan protested. 'I've got the saloon to think about.'

'You don't have to leave. In fact it'll be better if you sit tight until things blow over. You'll be in good with the local law because you sent the posse out to the ranch. All I want you to do is bust Toft out of jail and hide him until I work on the plan to grab Doyle's silver.'

'Ryker's in jail, too,' Donovan said.

Lannick's grin faded. 'How in hell did that happen?' he demanded.

'That army investigator, Moran, grabbed him. He's being taken back to the fort in the morning.'

'The hell he is! Send a couple of men to the jail before the posse returns and bust Ryker and Toft out. Get moving. That posse will be on its way back by now. Better still, let's you and me go bust them out. We'll make a better job of it than any hired help. Come on, we don't have much time.'

Donovan looked as if he wanted to object, but thought better of it and took a pistol out of the desk drawer, tucking it into the waistband of his pants as he stood up. Lannick was already at the door of the office, racked by impatience, and he clattered down the stairs.

They went along the back lots to the rear of the jail, where a window was situated in the wall of the jail kitchen. Lannick examined the window. He drew his pistol and shattered a pane of glass, then reached in and opened the window from the inside. He climbed into the kitchen and opened the back door.

'There might be a night jailer in the front office,' Donovan warned.

'It'll be his hard luck if there is,' Lannick said harshly. He cocked his gun and opened the door that led into the front office.

A townsman, Frank Johnson, was seated behind the

desk, his feet up on a second chair. His head was forward, chin on his chest, and he was snoring lustily. A double-barrelled shotgun was lying on the desk in front of him and his left hand rested lightly on the gleaming metal. Lannick went to Johnson's side and dealt him a ferocious blow to the head with the barrel of his pistol. Johnson relaxed into unconsciousness. Lannick jerked open the desk drawer and took out a keyring which had just two keys on it.

'Unlock that cage,' Lannick said, tossing the keys to Donovan.

'What are you doing back in town, Nick?' Ryker demanded, peering between the bars of the cage door.

'You might well ask,' Lannick countered. 'And what kind of trouble would you be in if I hadn't decided to return? There's been hell to pay this evening. Nothing has gone right, and you've made it a whole lot worse, running wild like you did. I told you to lay off, didn't I? Why can't you do like you're told, huh? Ain't I got enough to worry about without you making it ten times worse?'

'Let's get the hell out of here,' Donovan cut in. 'Save your family squabble for later.'

'So what's going on?' Ryker demanded.

'We're taking you and Toft out of here,' Lannick said. 'Because of what's happened this evening I'm gonna rearrange the big steal from Doyle's silver mine.'

'Toft won't be much good to you,' Ryker observed. 'He's got a fever from that bullet wound he collected, and he won't make much sense for a couple of days.'

'He'll be able to tell us where the silver's being held and about the setup; that will be good enough. Come on, rattle your hocks. Let's get moving.'

The street door was pushed open and a man, Joe Kelly, entered the office. He paused on the threshold and stared in shock at Lannick.

'What are you doing here?' he demanded. 'A posse has gone out to the CL looking for you. They said you stole a pile of Donovan's dough.' He broke off when he saw Donovan standing in the background and Ryker helping the semi-conscious Toft out of the prisoner cage. 'Heck, you're busting them out of jail!' he declared, and reached for the gun on his hip.

Lannick was holding his pistol, and, when Kelly cleared leather with his Colt, Lannick fired a shot which struck Kelly in the chest. Kelly twisted and fell to the floor, losing his hold on his gun as he went down. The thunder of the shot ripped through the silence and threw violent echoes across the office. Donovan ran to Lannick's side.

'You've done it now.' Shock sounded in his voice. 'That'll bring the whole town running. Let's get outa here.'

'He was gonna shoot me,' Lannick retorted, his face twisted into a mask of rage. 'What are you standing there for? Get Toft out the back door.'

'We can't take him to the saloon,' Donovan said. 'It'll be the first place they'll look.'

'Then where?' Lannick demanded.

'Henty's cabin on the edge of town will do,' Donovan rapped. 'Henty will keep him hidden until you need him.'

'What about me?' Jennings demanded, standing uneasily in the background.

'Come with us, and hurry it up. We're short of men at the moment.' Lannick went to Ryker's side, caught hold of

Toft, who was trying to pull away from Ryker, and dragged him roughly out of the office and into the kitchen. When Toft struggled, Lannick struck his wounded shoulder with the barrel of his pistol. Toft fell and lay motionless. Ryker cursed.

'Now we'll have to carry him,' he snarled. 'Give me a hand, Jennings.'

'So get to it,' Lannick said. 'Do you want the posse to come back and catch us in the act?'

Donovan led the way with Lannick at his side, and Ryker and Jennings carried Toft through the shadows. They gained the main street twenty yards from the law office and crouched in dense shadow in the doorway of a dress shop when the sudden clatter of hoofs alerted them to danger. The posse was returning. Lannick lifted his gun but remained motionless, watching as the riders reined up in front of the law office. He nudged Ryker and they picked up Toft again and continued on. A moment later cries of consternation erupted from the law office. Lannick urged Ryker to keep moving. For the moment, they were in the clear. . . .

Davis led the posse from the CL ranch on the way back to Grey Ridge. Moran reined up as soon as they were out of sight of the spread.

'What's wrong?' Davis demanded, twisting in his saddle.

'We're not going back to town immediately,' Moran said. 'I've got some bad feelings about this place. We know Lannick is prominent in this business, and he seems to be running the crookedness around town, so I figure he's linked up with others of his kind. Of course, my only interest in this is the deserters. There are at least half a dozen of them hanging around somewhere, and Jennings, now in jail, was riding into town when I picked him up. He didn't look as if he'd been living rough, so I figure he had himself a job on one of the ranches in the county, maybe the CL. If that is where he's got in then why have the rest of the deserters followed suit? What's the attraction? It can't be just working on a horse ranch. Anyway, that's how I figure it, and I've got to check it out. We'll stick around here until sunup and then look for prints. If someone rode out here ahead of us to warn them a posse was on its way, then we should find tracks left by the deserters when they pulled out.'

'That sounds OK,' Davis agreed, 'but we can't stay with you. I wanta get back to town and keep a close eye on things. I'm still trying to find out what happened to the sheriff.'

'I'll be as quick as I can and come back to take Ryker and Jennings off your hands in the morning,' Moran said.

'Good luck.' Davis held up a hand in farewell and then rode on with the posse.

Moran dismounted and began to unsaddle. 'You heard what I told the deputy, Sergeant,' he said to Braddock. 'We'll make camp here and be ready to start looking around at first light.'

'Yes, sir.' Braddock gave orders to the detail and they settled down quickly.

Moran was awake before the sun showed, and they were saddled and ready to ride as soon as the first shafts of sunlight cut across the eastern horizon.

'This won't take long,' Moran told the men. 'If we don't

find tracks then we'll head back to town, get some food, and take Ryker and Jennings to the fort. If we find any tracks that look promising we'll follow them to a conclusion, and in that case I'll send one of you to the fort to pick up some rations. OK, let's ride. We're looking for tracks leaving the CL ranch that might have been made last evening just before we showed up. We'll ride a circle around the place.'

Moran led the way, keeping just out of sight of the CL, and when they reached the rear of the spread he saw the tracks of about six horses riding out from the corral. He dismounted, and Braddock joined him to look at the prints with an experienced gaze.

'It looks like you've hit pay dirt, Captain,' Braddock mused. 'These prints are only a few hours old, and whoever rode out last evening sure was in a big hurry.'

'We'll follow them,' Moran decided. 'Let's push on now.'

They swung away from the ranch, following the tracks. The signs were that the group of riders had ridden fast to get clear of the ranch, for a mile or so later the prints showed that they had eased their mounts to a more leisurely pace. Two hours later, Moran, leading his detail by a few yards, eased to the crest of a low ridge and looked down on a water hole with a cabin situated nearby. A picket line strung out from the back of the cabin to a post had six horses tethered to it.

Moran saw two men sitting outside the cabin and hurriedly ducked back into cover. He signalled Braddock to join him as he took his field glasses out of a saddle-bag. When Braddock dismounted beside him, Moran cautioned silence and they eased up to the crest for Braddock to take a look at the cabin. Moran handed over his field glasses.

'You know the deserters,' he said. 'See if you can recognize either of those two men.'

Braddock adjusted the glasses to his sight and gazed at the cabin, swinging the glasses slowly. He pulled back suddenly and looked at Moran, a smile on his face.

'Those two down there are Troopers Smithson and Thompson, both posted as deserters, Captain.' Braddock said.

'They'll know you by sight so take your three men and ride around to the left of the cabin. I'll wait until you're in position and then ride in to challenge them. Cover me, and close in when I show myself. I don't think they'll surrender, so be ready for trouble.'

Braddock moved back from the crest and went off with his men. Moran watched them ride to the left, and when they were in position by the side of the cabin and hidden by the front corner of the little building Moran swung into his saddle, loosened his pistol in its holster and rode over the ridge and down the slope to the front of the cabin.

TEN

Deputy Sheriff Davis walked unsuspectingly into the law office when the posse reached town and pulled up short at the sight of the man lying dead on the threshold. Then he saw Johnson, the night jailer, unconscious at the desk. A glance at the prisoner cage showed that Ryker and Toft were no longer inside. Cawston was there, unconscious and snoring loudly. Davis knelt beside the body on the floor, recognized the dead man as Kelly, a townsmen, and shouted for one of the posse men outside to fetch the doctor. He went to the desk, and was relieved to find Johnson was still alive. He sat down on a corner of the desk and waited for the doctor to arrive.

Doc Harvey came hurrying into the office carrying his medical bag. He glanced at Kelly, inert on the threshold, shook his head and went to the desk to bend over the night jailer. He looked up at Davis, who was badly shocked.

'Who did this?' Harvey demanded.

'I don't know,' Davis replied. 'I found these two like this when we got in from the CL ranch. Ryker, the deserter Jennings and Toft are gone from the cage. Now who in hell would wanta bust those three out of here?'

'Captain Moran had a guard on Cahill, at my place, when Ryker was loose earlier,' Harvey mused. 'He suspected Ryker of wanting to kill Cahill. You'd better send a couple of your posse men over to my place to watch Cahill in case there's another attempt on him.'

'I'll do that right away.' Davis got up and went to the door. He called orders to the waiting posse men, and two of them rode to the doctor's house. Harvey called in two others to help carry the unconscious night jailer over to his office, and when they had departed, Davis slumped down at the desk, wondering just what he should do next.

Donovan led the way to Henty's cabin. Jennings and Ryker were carrying Toft now, and Lannick urged them to make haste. Henty opened the cabin door in response to Donovan's knock, and grinned at the sight of the saloon man, but his expression sobered when Lannick stepped into the doorway and entered, followed by Ryker and Jennings carrying the unconscious Toft.

'Say, what gives?' Henty demanded. 'What are they doing here? I did what you asked, boss. I just got back from CL.'

'Thanks,' Donovan said. 'I'll pay you for your trouble. Now I've got another favour to ask. Will you put these men up for a few days? They don't want to be seen around town.'

'I won't stay here,' Lannick said. 'I've got my own hidey-hole. I want to see these men taken care of before I leave, and I need to talk to Toft, if he's in a fit condition.'

Henty shrugged. 'It's OK by me,' he said. 'They'll have

to stay quiet, though, and no moving around. I don't want any trouble with the law.'

'I've got something I need to do before I settle down anywhere,' Ryker mused.

Lannick turned on him angrily. 'I don't want any more trouble around town,' he said harshly. 'Your personal problems will keep until after I've got what I want. I won't stand for any nonsense, so get that through your thick skull and remember it. We're gonna lift the silver from Doyle's mine; that'll set us up for the rest of our lives. Let's get that done and settled before you think about anything else. Now put Toft down on that bed. Henty, have you got some whiskey? I need to talk to Toft, so try and bring him round.'

'I'm going back to the hotel.' Donovan spoke with a trace of resignation in his voice. 'You can do this without me.'

'Don't worry.' Lannick grinned. 'I'll see you get your share of the silver.'

Donovan grimaced and departed. He walked back along the sidewalk towards the saloon, being careful not to be seen out at this particular hour.

Lannick took the whiskey bottle that Henty produced and tilted it to pour some of the liquid into Toft's mouth. Toft choked, coughed and opened his eyes.

'It's OK,' Lannick said. 'You're safe here. Do you feel like talking?'

'What do you wanta talk about?' Toft slurred his words. Sweat beaded his forehead. His face was pale, grey beneath the skin and his eyes were glassy with fever. 'All I want to do is roll over and die. You better get the doc in to look at me. I ain't feeling so good.'

'There's plenty of time for that,' Lannick said. 'Right now I want to know where Doyle is keeping his silver at the mine until he moves it to the bank because we're going right in there and take it from him. So get your mind working on the job and tell me where the stuff is and how much is salted away. You've been stalling me for days, Toft, and now I've got to act fast.'

Toft regarded him silently for some moments. His head lolled on his shoulders and he was having difficulty keeping his eyes open. He tried to moisten his lips, and when he spoke his voice was hoarse and trembling.

'I ain't been stalling,' he said in an undertone. 'Doyle has been mighty secretive about the silver. He ain't even told us in the office where he's keeping it. All I know is that it's in the mine somewhere, being guarded night and day. I run the mine office, but I never get the chance to go down into the workings. I do know Doyle has close to a hundred thousand dollars worth of silver cached underground.'

'Suppose we grab Doyle and force him to tell us where the silver is located?' Lannick mused.

'You don't know Doyle. He'd die before revealing where the silver is. I guess the only way to get it is to go into the mine and look for it. There are men guarding it so it's obvious they've got an old working cordoned off and are keeping a close eye on it.'

'You should have put more effort into locating the stuff,' Lannick said.

'I couldn't show too much interest in it,' Toft protested. 'When one of the clerks began to ask questions he was fired on the spot.'

'So if Doyle won't talk then who else knows where the silver is who can be forced to open up about it?' Lannick's eyes were cold as he gazed at the feverish Toft. 'There's got to be a weak link somewhere.'

'I hadn't thought about that,' Toft mused. 'Deke Hansen is Doyle's top security man. He'd know for sure where the silver's stashed, and I don't think he'll die to keep the secret. Grab him, put some pressure on him, and he might cave in. It could be worth a try at that.'

'Where do we drop on to Hansen and what does he look like?' Lannick asked.

'I know him,' Ryker cut in. 'I've played poker with him, He plays a mean game. But Toft could be right about him. He seems like a man who enjoys life too much to risk it trying to save somebody else's silver when the chips are down.'

'He lives in Doyle's house uptown, where the better houses are,' Toft said.

'Yeah, I've seen Doyle's house. Let me think about this and see what I can come up with.' Lannick grinned. 'It looks like we're getting somewhere now. I'll come back to you when I've worked out how we're gonna handle it.' His gaze rested on Ryker's face for a moment and then he sighed. 'I can read your mind,' he mused. 'The minute I turn my back you're going after Cahill and that gal. But you better forget it because I'll kill you if you mess up this deal I'm working on.'

'I'm not gonna do a thing until you've taken the silver,' Ryker said fervently.

Lannick shook his head and turned away, but paused when he reached the door.

'I've changed my mind,' he said. 'Pick up Toft and bring him along. I can't trust any of you, it seems, and I know just the place where I can keep an eye on you.'

Ryker knew better than to argue, and he and Jennings supported Toft and followed Lannick across the back lots towards the saloon. Lannick unlocked a door of the building next to the saloon and they entered. He lit a lantern and they looked around, finding themselves in a starkly furnished room with a steep ladder giving access to a trapdoor over their heads, the one leading to the big cupboard in Donovan's office.

Moran rode towards the cabin with his reins in his left hand, his right hand on his thigh close to the butt of his holstered pistol. The two men sitting in front of the cabin spotted him. One got to his feet immediately and went into the cabin. The other remained seated, but eased around to make his pistol easier to get at. Moran could see Braddock, dismounted now and followed by his detail, moving on foot to the front left-hand corner of the cabin.

The man who had gone into the cabin reappeared, followed by four others, who ranged themselves in a line in front of the cabin. Three were holding carbines at the ready, and Moran felt his nerves and muscles tense in anticipation of action. He moved forward until he was six yards from the cabin, and then halted his mount. One of the men stepped forward a pace, his hand on the butt of the pistol, snug in its holster on his right hip.

'Who in hell are you?' he challenged.

'I'm looking for the CL ranch,' Moran said. 'I've been told to ask for Tom Chivers.'

'What do you want with Chivers?'

'That,' Moran said, 'is between Chivers and me.'

'Well this ain't no horse ranch,' the spokesman said, and grinned.

'But it is a part of the CL ranch,' Moran said calmly. 'Where's the ranch house?'

'Why don't you get out of here and go look for it?' the man replied. 'Who in hell do you think you are, riding in like you own the place?'

Out of a corner of his eye, Moran saw Sergeant Braddock easing around the corner of the cabin, gun in hand.

'OK,' he said, 'I'll come clean. I'm Captain Moran of the Army Special Investigation Department and I'm hunting deserters from Fort Grant. I'm not here alone. I have an army detail with me, surrounding this place, and they have orders to shoot if any of you try to resist or escape. I know you six are deserters, and I call upon you to surrender. Put down your weapons and raise your hands.'

A shocked silence followed Moran's words, and he continued briskly: 'You all know Sergeant Braddock from Fort Grant. He's standing at the corner of the cabin now, covering you with his pistol. Take a look at him before you decide your course of action.'

Braddock stepped out into the open from around the corner as heads swivelled to look in his direction. His pistol was levelled in his hand. He grinned, motioning with his left hand, and the three tough soldiers of his detail also stepped forward to reveal themselves.

'I advise you to surrender,' Moran called.

The silence seemed intolerably heavy as the six men

considered Moran's ultimatum. The man who had elected himself spokesman made a nervous movement with his right hand towards his holstered gun, but stopped when he realized what he was doing. Moran waited calmly.

'Time's running out,' he announced. 'Drop your guns and we'll take you back to Fort Grant.'

'To hell with that! I ain't going back to the army. Let her rip, fellers! Start the play.'

The call from one of the men started the others into action. The man in front bent his elbow and clawed at the butt of his pistol. Moran set his hand into motion, pulling his gun quickly and smoothly, cocking it before he had levelled it. He triggered a shot into the chest of the man opposite. The other deserters then brought their weapons into play. Gun thunder blasted the silence and echoes hammered away across the wild terrain. Three of the deserters turned their attention to Braddock and the detail, and the remaining two lifted their guns against Moran even as the first deserter buckled at the knees and went down in a kicking heap with his pistol spilling from his hand.

Braddock fanned his pistol in a rapid tattoo of shots. Moran was fast enough to snap a shot at another of the deserters taking him on. The man lifted his carbine and triggered it swiftly as Moran fired. Moran dived sideways out of his saddle, hit the ground on his left shoulder, and kept his pistol in the aim. He saw his shot strike the deserter in the right shoulder. The man lost his grip on his long gun and dropped to his knees, his weapon falling aside. Blood spurted from his shoulder and he fell forward on to his face and lay still.

The three-man detail with Braddock proved up to their work. The shooting was thunderous and accurate, and climaxed as quickly as it had started. The deserters were blasted out of existence. The guns fell silent and Braddock came forward to check each man, throwing aside discarded weapons although their owners were past using them. The sergeant came to face Moran, saluted and made his report.

'All dead, Captain. They made their choice.'

'Leave them lying, Sergeant,' Moran replied. 'We'll send someone from the fort to clean up here. I want to get back to town as quickly as possible.'

Braddock shouted orders to his men, and three minutes later they were riding back the way they had come, leaving six lifeless bodies stiffening in the hot afternoon sunshine. Moran set a fast pace, concerned now about what might have happened in Grey Ridge during his absence. He felt that Deputy Sheriff Davis was not quite up to the job that had been thrust upon him by the sheriff's death, and he was concerned about Cahill and Laura Rivington. He was relieved when they eventually came in sight of the town, silent and brooding in the hot afternoon.

'It looks peaceful enough, Captain,' Braddock commented.

'Not too peaceful, I hope,' Moran replied. 'Let's look in at the law office.'

Moran rode along the street and dismounted in front of the office. He opened the door and peered inside. Davis was seated at the desk, and got to his feet when he saw Moran.

'I've been wondering how you were getting on,' Davis said. 'What happened?'

Moran told him. Davis shook his head wearily.

'I didn't think those deserters would come quietly. But there was trouble in town last night.' He explained about finding his prisoners gone.

Moran shook his head. 'Have you checked on Cahill and Miss Rivington?' he demanded.

'Don't worry about them,' Davis assured him. 'I've got a couple of men guarding them around the clock. There's been no sign of Ryker around town, and no one has seen anything of Lannick, either. It's been very quiet.'

'The calm before the storm,' Moran observed. 'Come with me and we might be able to make some progress.'

Davis nodded, eased his gunbelt and touched the butt of his holstered pistol. 'Lead on,' he said. 'Things always seem to happen when you take a hand. Where are we going?'

'I want another talk with Donovan. Let's see if we can shake him up.'

'Do you suspect him of anything crooked?'

'Someone entered the law office and busted out your prisoners,' Moran pointed out, 'and Donovan was thick with Lannick. I suspect Lannick of busting open the jail, and Donovan is the likeliest man in town to assist him. If we can get Donovan to tell us where Lannick is we can bring this business to a close.'

They left the office. Braddock and his detail were waiting outside. Moran sent them off to get a meal and some rest. Then he and Davis went along the boardwalk to the saloon. Moran pushed through the batwings and, followed closely by Davis, went to the bar where a bartender was washing glasses. Moran asked for Donovan and the bartender nodded.

'Mr Donovan is up in his office,' he said. 'And he doesn't want to be disturbed.'

'We won't keep him long,' Davis said.

Moran made his way through to the back the building and led Davis up the stairs to the office. Moran reached the office door, drew his pistol, paused for a moment, and then thrust the door open and stepped quickly into the office with Davis at his left elbow.

Donovan was seated at the desk. He looked up quickly at their intrusion. Two saddle-bags were on the desk – one was opened to reveal that it was packed with wads of paper money. Donovan gulped in shock when he recognized his visitors. His face expressed guilt, which was quickly replaced by anger. He got to his feet. Moran glanced towards the safe – its door was open wide.

'What the hell are you doing, busting in here like that?' Donovan demanded. 'You've got no right. You're breaking the law, Davis.'

Moran walked to the desk, his pistol covering Donovan, who dropped back into his seat, his expression turning sullen.

'It looks like we've caught you at a bad moment,' Moran observed. 'What do you think, Davis? You represent the law.'

'Is this the dough you said Lannick stole last evening?' Davis inquired, frowning.

'Lannick brought it back,' Donovan said.

'When?' asked Moran.

'Last night.' Donovan closed the flap of the saddle-bag.

Davis came to the desk and opened the bag again. He picked up a wad of greenbacks and looked at the wrapper around it, and then glanced at Moran. 'It says "Grey Ridge Miners' Bank" on this wrapper. I wouldn't mind betting this is some of the dough stolen when the bank was raided. It's brand new stuff, never been issued, by the look of it. I'll check with the bank for numbers of the missing notes. How'd you get hold of this cash, Donovan?'

'It's not all mine,' Donovan said tensely. 'Lannick must have put some of his money in with mine.'

'And he asked you to take care of his share, huh?' Davis asked.

'Donovan shrugged, and made no reply.

'You lied to me several times last evening,' Moran said. 'I think it's about time you came clean and told us what's going on. Where's Lannick? We believe he went along to the jail and busted out the prisoners after he dropped this money back here with you.'

'And you went with him.' Davis prompted. 'You better start talking before I get tough, Donovan. If you know what's good for you then you'll spill the beans. The sheriff was murdered last night and someone is gonna pay for that with a rope around his neck. I can't see Lannick taking the blame for it, so it looks like you've been elected.'

'Don't try to pin that killing on me,' Donovan said sharply. 'It was Lannick shot Appleby. They were in cahoots for months, until Appleby got too greedy.'

'And where is Lannick now?' Davis demanded.

'Right here,' Lannick said from across the room.

Moran swung around to see Lannick emerging from the big cupboard in the corner. He was holding a pistol, the muzzle pointing at Moran's chest. Moran waited, unmoving. But Davis was not covered, and the deputy reached for his gun in a surprisingly fast draw. Lannick caught the movement from a corner of his eye and swung his pistol towards Davis. Moran triggered his gun instantly. Lannick jerked under the lightning fast strike of a bullet in his chest. He managed to get off a shot but was already falling over backwards with blood spilling from his wound. His bullet smacked into the desk and Donovan fell off his seat.

The crash of the shots shook the room. Davis ran to Lannick and kicked the discarded gun away into an opposite corner.

'He came out of that cupboard,' Davis said as the gun echoes began to fade.

Moran was already closing in on the cupboard, his gun ready. The cupboard door stood ajar, and Moran caught a glimpse of movement from within. He shouted a warning to Davis and hurled himself aside as a tongue of muzzle flame spurted from inside the cupboard. A figure moved into the doorway and a gun fired again, filling the office with smoke. Davis fired twice and Jennings lurched forward out of the cupboard and dropped to his knees, a gun spilling from his hands. He fell forward on to his face and lay still. Moran ran into the cupboard, saw the ladder and peered down into the room below.

A man was standing halfway up the ladder, holding a gun. He was looking up, and called out when he saw Moran, not recognizing him.

159

'What's going on, Jennings?'

Moran recognized Ryker's voice. 'It's all over, Ryker,' he replied. 'This is Captain Moran. Drop that gun and come up here. I've got you covered.'

Ryker squeezed his trigger without hesitation and the bullet tore through the wide brim of Moran's hat. The flash of the shot dazzled Moran but he fired instantly and the bullet struck Ryker in the forearm, causing him to drop his gun, which fell into the room below. Ryker fell off the ladder, dropped eight feet, and landed on his back. His head struck the floor and his senses fled. Moran clattered down the ladder and covered the wounded Toft.

Davis came down the ladder, looking around. 'Lannick's dead,' he said, 'and the shot he fired when you hit him passed through Donovan's neck. I think he's dead, too.'

'Ryker's alive, and that's good,' Moran said. 'He'll be able to tell us what's been going on around here. Put him back in your jail. I want to pass on some good news to Cahill and Laura Rivington, and then perhaps I'll be able to get back to the chore that brought me here in the first place.'

Moran opened the door to the alley and went outside, took a deep breath of the clean air. A sigh of relief escaped him as he made his way to the doctor's house, thinking that it would be a pleasure to vindicate Lieutenant Cahill and restore him to his former reputation and way of life.